The
POLYESTER
GRANDPA

ALSO BY MARTHA FREEMAN

The Year My Parents Ruined My Life
Stink Bomb Mom

The
POLYESTER
GRANDPA

Martha Freeman

Holiday House/New York

Library of Congress Cataloging-in-Publication Data
Freeman, Martha, 1956–
The polyester grandpa / by Martha Freeman.—1st ed.
p.   cm.
Summary: When her prim and proper grandmother shows up with a
boisterous new husband, ten-year-old Molly and her mother really
dislike him, but after a series of confrontations, they learn to see
both him and themselves in a new light.
ISBN 0–8234–1398–5
[1. Family life—Fiction.   2. Grandparents—Fiction.   3. Snobs and
snobbishness—Fiction.]   I. Title.
PZ7.F87496Po   1998   98-15815   CIP   AC
[Fic]—dc21

For the grandmas and the grandpas—
Herman and Nettie Frank
Barbara Freeman and Julian Neistadt
Leslie and Susan Freeman

Acknowledgments

The author wishes to thank her friend and neighbor Dr. Mary Lindholm, the veterinarians of Centre Animal Hospital and State College Veterinary Hospital, and Persian-cat breeder Pat Frey for their help. Any mistakes are, of course, the author's.

The
POLYESTER
GRANDPA

Chapter One

The first I heard about my new grandpa was the thump from the kitchen.

"Mommy! Are you okay?" My little brother, the nuisance, sounded scared.

I dropped Regina's brush and ran to investigate. *Holy moly!* Mom was flat on the kitchen floor.

I bent down to check if she was breathing. Yes!

I got next to her ear and yelled "Mommy!" right in it. I haven't called her Mommy in a thousand zillion years, but I was scared. It wasn't till her eyes blinked open that I started breathing again myself.

Meanwhile, the nuisance had gotten a glass of water. He started to dump it on her face, but I grabbed his wrist. Only about half the water sloshed.

The way Mom shrieked and burbled, though, you would have thought the whole thing spilled on her.

I took the glass away, but the nuisance tried to wrestle me for it. He wanted to pour the rest. "Yosemite Sam did it when Bugs Bunny wouldn't wake up," he argued.

"They are cartoon characters, *okay*?"

"Excuse me." Mom had raised herself up to lean on her elbows. Water dripped off her nose. "If you two aren't busy, could I have a towel?"

"What happened, anyway?" I handed her a towel. Mom is always getting hyper over something. But this was the first time she had ever actually fainted.

"I was sorting the mail, and . . . oh!" Mom had spotted a picture postcard that lay on the floor. She made a face, then leaned over and picked it up by the corner, like a wet diaper.

"Is that what made you faint?" I asked.

Without looking at it, she nodded and gave it to me. It was pretty yuk-o all right. Not yuk-o enough that I wanted to faint, but pretty yuk-o. The photo showed a pink heart-shaped bed with a bottle of champagne on its pink heart-shaped pillows.

I flipped it over and read:

Dear Lila, Don, and Children,
  Surprise!
  Jimmy and I were married Thursday, and we've been honeymooning ever since!
  We plan to be at your house Wednesday, so get the guest room ready!
  Love,
  Grandma
P. S. Do you have any silk sheets?

"Oh, my stars in heaven!" I said it just the way Grandma does. "Who's Jimmy?"

The nuisance, who is four, was tugging at my blouse. He didn't want to be left out. "What happened? What's it say?"

I told him.

"But grandmas can't get married," he answered.

I ignored him, even though I sort of agreed. "What about Grandfather?"

"Grandfather, indeed," Mom said. She talks like that. Before she became a professional homemaker, she was a professional English professor. "He's only been gone a year, may he rest in peace. Your grandmother *might* have waited." She reached for the kitchen counter and slowly pulled herself up.

"Aren't you gonna faint anymore?" The nuisance was still disappointed he didn't get to pour the rest of the water, I could tell.

Mom smiled weakly. "I think I'm done for today."

"Have you met whatsisname—" I looked back at the postcard. "Jimmy?"

"No, I haven't," Mom said. "She told me he had invited her to lunch. I didn't think it was such a short distance from a sandwich to the altar."

I shook my head. Holy moly. This must be really weird for Mom. I mean, if I found out all of a sudden *she* was married to a guy named Jimmy, I'd probably faint, too.

Mom stood there looking out the kitchen window at the woods in back of our house. There were wrinkles around her eyes—either mad wrinkles or worry wrinkles, I couldn't tell which. Seeing her like that, I almost wished we were a huggy kind of family, like my friend Stephanie's. Then I could put my arms around her. But in my family, a ten-year-old like me is a bit grown-up for that sort of thing.

"Do you feel better now?" I finally asked.

"Except for a mild case of pneumonia," she said, "from my damp clothes." She narrowed her eyes at the nuisance, but she was teasing, which meant she felt better. Mom's like that—goes from mood to mood fast. She told me once it's because she took too many drama classes where you have to pretend you're happy, then sad, then mad, then scared—one right after the other. After a while, she said, you don't know how you really feel anymore.

"You can go back to Regina," Mom said to me. "Your homework's done, right?"

"Of course, Mom. It's almost four-thirty."

"Just checking. Anyway, I'm going to get to work on the *poulet sauté* for dinner."

"Poo-lay what?" the nuisance asked. He looked worried.

I didn't blame him. When I was little, my mom's gourmet food tasted like poison to me, too. Especially anything with wine in it. Yuk-*o*! But now I'm sort of used to it. Plus, I'm learning French.

"'Poulet' is 'chicken,'" I whispered. "'Sauté' is sort of like 'fried.'"

"Fried chicken?" His face lit up.

Mom took out the cleaver. *Rap-rap-rap-rap-rap.* She started chopping a little brown thing. It smelled like an onion. I think it was a shallot. There was a bunch of green leaves on the cutting board, too. Tarragon? It wasn't going to be the kind of fried chicken the nuisance had in mind. "Don't get your hopes up," I told him.

While Mom chopped, she talked to herself. "They're arriving Wednesday—that's tomorrow, for heaven's sake. So after dinner, I'll launder the guest-room sheets. *Cotton* sheets. And no heart-shaped pillows, either."

She was chopping furiously now. I wondered if she was thinking of that Jimmy guy. "You're sure you don't need me?" I asked. I was afraid she might fall over again—or cut her fingers off.

"No, no, Molly, I'm fine." She waved the cleaver at me. "*Really.* I'm sure we'll all get along beautifully with Jimmy. Can't wait to meet him. *Really.*"

"Well . . . okay, then."

Rap-rap-rap-rap-rap.

The nuisance trailed me back to Regina's room. Usually, I hate having him around because usually he messes stuff up. Like the time he knocked over a can of Regina's chalk and it went everyplace. I had to vacuum forever.

You can see why I call him the nuisance instead of his real name, which is Joe. But for some reason, Regina likes him. She sleeps on his bed all the time, never on mine. This is one of the mysteries of my life.

And now I had a new mystery, a huge one: Why did my grandmother go off and marry somebody I never heard of? I mean, I didn't even know his last name. What was I supposed to call him? Not Grandfather. There could never be another Grandfather.

All these thoughts were spinning in my head when I walked through Regina's door. Then I looked on her grooming table, and my thoughts went *poof.*

Holy moly! Regina was gone.

Chapter Two

I shouldn't have been surprised.

Regina is a pedigreed Persian. One day she'll be a champion, at least in the premiere division. That's for cats that aren't going to be dads or moms. With their long hair, Persians need a lot of grooming. And champion Persians need an extra lot. But even though I've read every book and I do everything exactly right, Regina does not like to be groomed.

Anyway, I must have left the door cracked open when I went to see about Mom. Regina had taken her chance and escaped.

"You look in your room and the linen closet. I'll try around here," I told the nuisance.

"Yes, Your Majesty!" The nuisance bowed and started for the stairs. He thinks he's terribly funny.

I looked behind the drapes, on the kitty gym, and inside the kitty condominium. Then I started on the rest of the downstairs, calling, "Here, kitty, kitty."

I was about to check the silver cupboard when Daddy opened the front door, and I saw a flash of white fluff by his shin.

"Howdy—" Daddy began. He was going to kiss me hello, but I had no time for that stuff. In another second, Regina would be hiding in the shrubs. So I pushed Daddy out of the way, hurdled over his briefcase, and made a diving lunge off the porch.

"Ha! Got you!"

Of course, I was careful not to squeeze too hard or put any weight on her. I couldn't afford bruises, since her very first Cool-Cat Cat Show was happening that Sunday. So when I sat up and saw all the blood, I wasn't worried. I knew it was my own.

"Molly! Honey! You poor thing—let me get bandages, antiseptic, oh dear. . . ." Unlike Mom, Daddy is usually a calm kind of person. But he doesn't do well with two things: heights and blood.

"It's just my nose." I tilted my head back and sniffled. Yuk-*o*. "I bonked it on the step, I guess. Could you take Regina, though? I don't want her fur to get stained."

I held her out and felt Daddy remove her squirming body from my arms. "Come on— *ouch!*—Your Long-tailed Highness."

With my head tilted back, I couldn't see if he was holding her right. "Don't hurt her," I warned him. "The Cool-Cat Cat Show—"

"—is only five days away. I know, Molly. We *all* know. I wouldn't dream of—*ow!*—hurting her."

Staring upward, I went back into the house. Daddy closed Regina in her room, got an ice pack from the kitchen, then met me in the downstairs bathroom.

"My poor princess." He dabbed my face with a washcloth.

"I'm fine, Daddy. It's just a bloody nose."

He gulped and made a face. "Awfully messy."

"Are you sure you want to do that? I can—"

"Daddy-Daddy-Daddy!" The nuisance ran in and grabbed him around the knees. "Didja hear about Jimmy? Our new grandpa? Mom died! But I splashed her, and—"

"Slow down, Joey." Daddy stopped dabbing. "What's he talking about, anyway?"

Mom came in. The bathroom was getting crowded. "Are you okay, Molly? Here, Don, I'll do that." She took the washcloth from Daddy.

"What's this Joe's saying about grandpas?" Daddy asked.

"*Big* news." Mom raised her eyebrows. "Details at dinner. Now, why don't you and Joe go check the hollandaise sauce? If it curdles, I swear, I shall give up cooking forever."

The nuisance believed her. "Ya-a-a-ay!"

"Don't count on it," said Daddy. Seeing Mom's face, he added, "Just kidding, hon."

When they were gone, Mom smiled at me. "Your dad was looking a tad bit green. One of us fainting is plenty. Okay, good as new," she pronounced. Then she mumbled to herself, "Now let me just run a mop over this floor, and then I'll get back to the wild-rice pilaf."

The floor looked spotless to me, but Mom is a nut about having a clean house. Daddy says she was a slob when she was busy being a professional professor, but I can't picture it.

After I changed my blouse, I went back to Regina. I still had to bathe her and brush her. Mom said she'd wait dinner, but if the rice got mushy it would be my fault.

I was fixing Regina's harness so she'd stay in the kitty sink, when the nuisance came up beside me. "Go away," I told him.

"Aw, come on, Molly. Lemme help."

I rolled my eyes but let him stay while I soaked Regina. She glared at me. Sometimes I think washing makes her mad because she's embarrassed. A Persian cat is mostly fur. When it's wet, what's left is this scrawny, pinkish thing. Not very beautiful.

"Shampoo," I ordered.

The nuisance handed it to me. "Shampoo."

I rubbed Regina till the soap foamed up. "Do you remember Grandfather very well?" I asked. I was thinking how a year is a long time when you're only four.

"Course I 'member 'im," the nuisance said.

"Spray deal. And be *careful.*"

He picked it up by the hose so it wouldn't squirt. "Spray deal."

I rinsed Regina, who kept right on glaring. "Humectant."

"Hu-mo . . . whatever-you-call-it."

"Hu-mec-tant," I said. "It's conditioner for cats. What do you remember?"

"How mean he was."

I was so surprised, I dropped the bottle. The thump made Regina yowl. "Sorry." I stroked her.

"Almost done." Then I looked down at the nuisance. "What do you *mean* 'mean'?"

"Well, he was. 'Member when I picked that flower? He yelled at me."

I did remember. Grandfather had been an anesthesiologist. That's a doctor who makes people go to sleep so another doctor can cut them open. After he retired, he raised these pink roses. Every year he entered them in the flower show, and every year they won a blue ribbon.

I tried to explain this to the nuisance. "He wasn't mean. It's just that those flowers were important. Grandfather won prizes with them."

"Like you're gonna do with Regina?"

"Well, yeah. It is like that. I mean, he took care of those flowers the same way I take care of Regina—"

"He *washed* 'em?"

"No, he didn't *wash* 'em. But he watered 'em. And fertilized 'em. And . . . well, killed all the bugs, I guess."

The time Grandfather yelled at the nuisance, we were staying at my grandparents' house for the weekend while Mom and Dad were gone someplace. We were all outside in the rose garden. Grandma picked the crying nuisance up, wiped his eyes and nose on her handkerchief, and gave

Grandfather this real stern look that meant: "*Now, see what you've done.*"

Then she carried the nuisance into the house, while I tagged along after them, making faces to cheer Joe up. He was really little. He could hardly even talk yet. How was he supposed to know the roses were special?

Grandma kept a shelf of storybooks by the window seat in her room. They had been her books when she was little. She pulled out *The Emperor's New Clothes,* and pretty soon the nuisance and I were both laughing.

Now, I could hardly believe the nuisance remembered it at all. It made me sad to think that's how he thought of Grandfather.

And anyway, he was wrong. Grandfather wasn't mean. He was just—I searched for the right word and came up with one Mom uses—"aloof." It's sort of the opposite of cuddly. Would Jimmy be like that, too? It made sense that he would be. Aloof must be the kind of guy Grandma liked.

"Blow-dryer," I said.

"Blow-dryer," the nuisance echoed.

I switched it on and aimed it. Regina, like always, closed her eyes and shrank as small as she could get. To her, the blow-dryer must be like a tornado. But it's what you put up with if you're cat royalty. Part of the deal.

I know all about putting up with stuff. We're not exactly royalty, but our last name *is* Knight. And Mom says her side of the family has always been smart; "accomplished" is her word for it. So even though I don't exactly love school, I'm expected to put up with it, work hard, get straight As.

If you're Molly Knight, it's part of the deal.

By now, Regina was fluffy again. "Kitty brush," I said to the nuisance.

"Kitty brush. Hey, Molly, can I be done helping? I'm hungry."

"Well, of course, you can be done! Who wanted you in the first place?"

He didn't say anything, just toddled off toward the kitchen.

"Hey, nuisance?"

He looked around. "What?"

"Thanks. You were a good helper."

The nuisance has a great grin. It's almost worth saying something nice just to see it. And anyway, it isn't completely his fault he's a nuisance. Everybody's four years old sometime, even Grandfather. I bet he was the only four-year-old in history who had perfect table manners.

I started in with the kitty brush. Two hundred strokes. My hand used to get tired, but now I'm used to it. Plus, it's a good time to think.

Even if he was aloof, even if he did yell at the nuisance once, I loved my grandfather. My clearest memories of him were from Christmastime. Before he died, we would always drive out to my grandparents' house for Christmas dinner. I could still see him carving the turkey. He seemed so important. And even though he was old, he was handsome—tall with silver hair. Mom used to say he could have been a movie star, except he was too smart. When he smiled at me, I felt proud to be part of the same family.

"One hundred three . . . one hundred four . . . one hundred five . . ."

After Grandfather died, Grandma sold their house and moved down to Florida. Mom was sad, even though she said it was the best thing. Last year at Christmas, Grandma came to visit us. But it wasn't a bit the same. I even caught Mom crying in the kitchen. She said it was because the rolls were flat, but I think really she missed her dad.

When I got to two hundred strokes, I took out the comb and ran it under Regina's legs, chin, and tail. Then, finally, I let her go. She did what she always does, leaped on top of her kitty condo and scratched like crazy. Meanwhile, I raked the comb through the brush to clean out the fur.

"Dinnertime!" Mom called.

I closed my eyes and tried to picture a grown man with a little-kid name standing next to my grandmother, who always wears dresses and heels and pearl earrings—even to eat breakfast. I tried as hard as I could, but the only person I could imagine standing there was my tall, handsome grandfather.

Chapter Three

Mom told Daddy all about the postcard at dinner.

"You actually *fainted,* hon?" Daddy cut a bite of chicken.

"Well . . . maybe not precisely," Mom said.

"You were on the floor!" The nuisance was using his fork to build a rice mountain. "Can I have a graham cracker?"

"I *was* surprised," Mom said. "But maybe I exaggerated the fainting part, just a tiny bit."

Daddy got up to get the graham crackers.

"You mean like a drama-class smile?" I asked.

She looked embarrassed.

"Mo-o-o-o-om." I shook my head. "Don't *do* that!"

"You're right, Molly. I'm sorry. But there's no need to worry. I don't expect to be that surprised ever again."

Daddy came in from the kitchen. "Anyway, hon, I think it's terrific. About Grandma, I mean. Best thing that could happen."

"You do?" Mom looked relieved.

"Sure. This Jimmy guy, he's gotta be a class act, right? Nothing less for your mother. And if they're happy, what could be bad?"

"But it's so *abrupt*—"

"Hey, at her age, what's she waiting for?"

Calming Mom down is one of Daddy's jobs around the house—like making breakfast Saturday mornings.

At work, Daddy's a CFO. He used to be a CPA. Exactly what those letters mean is one of the mysteries of my life. The best I can figure out, he adds and subtracts money all day. For a hobby he collects stamps. These are both terribly boring things to do. He told me once it's good he married a hyper person like Mom because they balance each other out. CFOs worry lots about whether things balance out.

I was clearing the table when the doorbell rang. It had to be Stephanie. She only lives a couple blocks down, so it's easy for her to walk over here.

"Hairy at your house, huh?" I let her in.

"*Oh* yeah." She rolled her eyes. "The 'rents are steamed 'cause Emily sneaked out with that guy again, Jerry."

Emily is Stephanie's teenage sister, and she's always getting yelled at. The worst was the time she came home with a rose tattooed on her shoulder blade.

I swear, I'm *never* going to be a teenager.

Like I said before, Stephanie's family is huggy. But they're also terribly loud. So when Stephanie can't take any more, she comes here. She says we're quiet, and I guess that's true. When somebody in my family is mad, they mostly glare. If it's really bad, they stomp around.

"Wanna watch a movie?" I asked.

"You are *so* lucky you don't have to do dishes."

"Yeah, but *you* don't get in trouble if you miss one single, tiny letter on the spelling test. Mom says the house is her profession, and mine is school."

"And Regina," Stephanie added.

I flopped into the beanbag chair in the family room and told her the big news about Jimmy and Grandma.

"Weird," she said. "And they're coming tomorrow? What if you hate him? What if he hates *you*?"

I hadn't thought of that. But grown-ups don't usually hate me. I'm one of those good kids, the kind that says please and thank you. According to Stephanie, it's pathetic.

Stephanie scanned the movie shelves. "*Cheez-itz*, Molly. How come you don't have any *normal* videos?"

"Like you don't already know. Mom doesn't believe in normal ones."

Stephanie sighed. "And she doesn't believe in TV. I could be home, watching *America's Most Wanted*—if I could hear it over the yelling. Anyway, this one sounds okay. *Night Must Fall*?"

She popped it in, but after a few seconds she asked, "What's the matter with it? Where's the colors?" Before I could stop her, she leaned forward and messed with the dials. The picture went totally kerflooey.

"Holy moly, Steph. It's in black and white! It's *old*! Now you've wrecked it."

"I can fix it, I can fix it." She twisted the dials back the other way. Somehow the picture straightened out.

The movie turned out to be terribly scary. This old lady is sick, and a young guy comes to take care of her. He's really, really sweet—too sweet. After a while we figure out he's been strangling all the neighbors, and next he's going to strangle her.

Daddy had been reading to the nuisance, and at the absolutely scariest part he came in to tell us it was bedtime. But he made the mistake of sitting down, and in a minute he had to find out if the old lady was going to get strangled, too. The movie was just ending when Stephanie's parents called to say come home.

The old lady didn't get strangled. But that didn't help the dead neighbors any. I practically couldn't sleep, thinking about it, and I woke up in the dark with my thoughts all jumbled: Some guy named Jimmy was on *America's Most Wanted* because he strangled old ladies. . . .

"Molly, are you all right?" The nuisance was standing next to my bed, staring right into my face.

"Yeah . . . wha—?"

"I heard you talking."

"Oh . . . sorry . . . I'm okay now."

"You sure? You need water, or—?"

"Poured in my face? No"—I yawned—"thanks. Go back to bed."

Chapter Four

At 4:30 the next afternoon, the nuisance and I were sitting in the living room, trying not to get wrinkled.

Mom had made us put on good clothes for my grandmother and "the groom," as she now called him. And Mom had gotten dressed up, too. Usually, she is terribly L. L. Bean, which is a mail-order store that sells the world's most boring clothes. A shirt is really exciting if it has pictures of wood ducks all over it. Mom says she dresses that way because everybody did at her boarding school. She can't get out of the habit.

Anyway, today I almost couldn't get my fractions done because she kept asking my opinion on different outfits. Finally, she found a purple dress in some way-back part of her closet. I said it looked like something a man named Jimmy would appreciate, so that's what she decided to wear.

While we waited, Mom paced the front hallway with a dustcloth in her hand. Every few steps, she stopped and wiped off a shelf or a picture frame.

I was trying to read the latest issue of *Purrfect Cat,* but I couldn't concentrate on "Treating Unsightly Stud Tail." For one thing, every time I got comfortable, Mom looked over and told me to "sit like a lady."

If waiting was hard on me and Mom, it was murder on the nuisance. He was sitting in a straight chair with his hands folded. He looked like he was about to burst.

It made me feel so bad, I offered to read him a book. But before I could get one, the doorbell rang. The nuisance and I looked at each other. Mom stopped pacing. I think for a second, the earth might have stopped rotating.

Then the nuisance bounced up and ran for the door, yelling, "I wanna see 'im first! I wanna see 'im first!"

He was fast, but Mom was faster. I decided to be dignified, so I took a deep breath and smoothed my skirt.

By the time I got to the door, my grandmother was trying to kiss my mother's cheek, and the nuisance was jumping up and down between them. Regina must have heard the door open. She was right there, ready to make her escape.

Where was Jimmy?

I stood on tiptoe and saw a wide, colorful something on the porch behind my grandmother. I was trying to figure out what or who it could be when—*not again!*—Regina ran for it. I couldn't get through the crowded doorway, so I yelled, "Grab 'er!" hoping Mom would scoop her up.

But Mom was so tangled in hellos that Regina was through her legs before she could move. The next thing I knew, a man's voice was saying, "Gotcha, ya little furball—*ow!* She's a nasty one, isn't she?" And Grandmother was giggling—*giggling!*—and the colorful something was turning out to be a short, fat man in a Hawaiian shirt, who was now holding my pedigreed Persian in his arms.

I was so surprised, I didn't even move when the man held her out.

This *couldn't* be Jimmy, the tall, handsome, aloof man my grandmother had married . . . ? But then, who was it? My thoughts were spinning.

The short, fat man sneezed, and my grandmother said, "Put the cat down, sweetie. We don't want your allergy acting up."

"Well, I'm tryin' to hand the kitty to its rightful owner, but she don't seem to want it. Yoo-hoo, Missy? Earth to Little Missy?"

Suddenly, I realized I was gawking, and I made my brain click back on: Close mouth, take cat, move tongue. "She's a pedigreed Persian," I said weakly. Regina squirmed, but I held her tight till the door was closed.

"My mistake, then. Her teeth are as sharp as any furball's, though. That I can tell you." The man my grandmother had just called "sweetie" sneezed again. Then he pulled a green-checkered handkerchief from his pocket, wiped his nose, and stuffed the handkerchief back in. When he grinned at me, I was too surprised to smile back.

I looked around one more time, in case the real Jimmy was hiding someplace.

But then I saw the way my grandmother's face beamed when she looked down at the fat man's bald head. "Jimmy," she said, "this is my ten-year-old granddaughter, Molly. Molly, this is Jimmy Barkenfalt, my husband."

"Ten years old, eh? Pretty girl like you must

have a boyfriend, am I right?" The man patted my shoulder and laughed like he had just said something terribly original.

Holy moly.

Chapter Five

My grandmother and Jimmy Barkenfalt finally made it through the door and, after about a thousand zillion trips, their suitcases got hauled upstairs to the guest room. Now they and the nuisance and I were all sitting in the living room, while Mom made iced tea in the kitchen.

Grandma and Jimmy Barkenfalt sat side by side on the sofa, and every now and then she fanned him with *Purrfect Cat*. He had done most of the luggage hauling, so he looked terribly sweaty.

I was still too stunned to talk, but the nuisance was doing a good job filling up silence. Between sniffles and wiping his nose on his hand, he was telling how at preschool Ethan J., world's biggest bully, hogged the new magenta crayon.

Grandmother smiled at him while she fanned, but I could tell she wasn't paying attention. Jimmy Barkenfalt, though, was nodding like he meant it. When the nuisance told how he had to sock Ethan J., Jimmy Barkenfalt positively exploded in laughter. "That's a good one, son. Don't let 'em push ya around."

The nuisance likes it when somebody listens to him. So he told how he had to go sit in the quiet corner, which wasn't fair because it was Ethan J. who wouldn't share. "Ain't that the way, Joe? No justice," said Jimmy Barkenfalt. "I remember one time when I had to wear a dunce cap, and I wasn't any dumber'n the other fellas. You want to hear about that?"

The nuisance nodded, and Jimmy Barkenfalt started telling a long, confusing story.

Holy moly. He wasn't tall. He wasn't handsome. And the way he treated the nuisance, he wasn't aloof, either.

Mom stayed in the kitchen so long, I thought she'd gone to Alaska for ice. Jimmy Barkenfalt had been as big a surprise to her as to me, I could tell. When she'd shaken hands with him, she'd laughed like she was thrilled, and smiled a huge smile. Then, when she turned away from him, the smile stayed right there on her face like she had forgotten about it.

The story Jimmy Barkenfalt was telling must have been confusing for my grandmother, too. She stopped fanning and looked over at me. "We've been having such fun," she said. "Yesterday, he took me to one of those little carnival parks by the shore. We ate cotton candy, and then we went through the Tunnel of Love!" She giggled.

This was the second time Grandma had giggled since she and Jimmy Barkenfalt got here. As far as I knew, it was the second time she had giggled in her whole life. My mouth tried to fall open again, but I caught it in time.

"Tunnel of Love," I echoed.

I had to admit she looked even prettier than usual. Really happy. And she was dressed a little differently, too. Instead of pearls, she was wearing some kind of flower-shaped earrings. Her dress was light blue and short enough to show her knees. She had on sandals instead of the usual high heels.

I looked over at short, fat, bald, sweaty Jimmy Barkenfalt, still telling about the time his teacher gave him a dunce cap. His shirt, stretched out over his belly, was pink with little palm trees on it. The skin on his legs was white.

I tried to picture him with Grandma in the Tunnel of Love, but it made me embarrassed. Just then, Jimmy Barkenfalt leaned over and gave Grandma a huge smooch on the lips. I might have fainted like Mom did yesterday, but I'll never know because behind me I heard a gasp, then *CRASH-clatter-clatter-clatter-SMASH.*

"Oh, my stars in heaven!" said my grandmother.

When I turned my head, Mom was standing in a puddle of iced tea. One hand covered her mouth and the other held a tipped tray, so it was no mystery what had happened. But Mom stared down at the ice cubes, lemon slices, and broken glass like they had dropped from outer space.

Jimmy Barkenfalt was already on his feet. "Here—lemme get that." Before the rest of us even moved, he was mopping up, then sweeping up.

"Isn't he wonderful?" my grandmother whispered.

I nodded, but I bet I had the same blank expression Mom did. He *was* wonderful, I guess. I mean, here he was cleaning up my mom's mess, and my grandmother was so happy, she actually giggled, and the nuisance was practically ready to climb onto his lap.

So how come I was starting to hate him?

Chapter Six

Everybody sort of gave up on iced tea after that. Mom disappeared into the kitchen to work on dinner. Grandma and Jimmy Barkenfalt went upstairs to unpack, with the nuisance tagging along behind. Me, I started the daily search for Regina.

I tried the bathroom and the kitty condo before I thought of the Tupperware cupboard, which is under the sink in the kitchen. Sometimes the nuisance leaves it open, and Regina dashes in for a nap.

The Tupperware cupboard is the only thing in our entire house Mom doesn't keep terribly sterile and organized. Actually, it's a complete mess. There are plastic tubs thrown one way, lids thrown another way, and bags from the grocery store wadded up everyplace.

Once Mom told me the Tupperware cupboard is a symbol for her subconscious mind. I think she meant that deep down, she's a slob, the way Daddy says she used to be when she was a professional English professor. If that's true, maybe it's unhealthy for her to keep the house so neat. I mean, is one part of her always fighting with the other part? So no wonder she's hyper.

I opened the cupboard door and knelt down. Sure enough, Regina's eyes glowed at me from the back corner. I reached in, wondering why my cat is so dumb she never figures out to close her eyes when she's trying to hide.

"Come on, 'furball.' "

Rap-rap-rap-rap-rap. Mom was chopping something again. I stood up and saw a bunch of leeks. And there were potatoes in the sink. So that meant vichyssoise, which is pronounced "vishy-swawz," in case you don't know—and I don't know why you would know unless your mom or dad is a gourmet cook, too. I guessed that must be dinner, in which case the nuisance would be eating graham crackers again.

"Is your homework done?"

"Of course, Mom."

"When you're finished with Regina, would you have a minute to help me? I'm getting anxious about time. The soup still has to chill."

"Okay." I was surprised. She almost never asks for help.

I carried Regina into her room. Even though Mom needed me, I couldn't rush Regina's grooming. Not with the Cool-Cat Cat Show so close. I only wash her twice a week, so today I started right in with the brush.

One . . . two . . . three . . .

While I counted, I tried to convince myself to like Jimmy Barkenfalt. After all, it really didn't matter what he looked like. Maybe I'd be fat someday, too.

Probably not bald though.

Fifty-one . . . fifty-two . . . fifty-three . . .

And it really didn't matter that he wore ugly clothes, either. Maybe it wasn't that he had terrible taste. Maybe he was color blind. That would be like a disability, and it isn't fair not to like somebody because of a disability.

One hundred twenty-six . . . one hundred twenty-seven . . . one hundred twenty-eight . . .

And really, wasn't it good that he kissed Grandma? Even if he did go and do it right on our sofa in front of everybody. It shouldn't be any big deal that old people kiss each other. Or eat cotton candy. Or go in the Tunnel of Love.

One hundred fifty-three . . . one hundred fifty-four . . . one hundred fifty-five . . .

And so what if Jimmy Barkenfalt said "ain't?" Those things don't matter as much as what's in your heart. Even Mom says that.

My thoughts spun round and round. I really did try to convince myself.

But I couldn't do it. Something about Grandma and Jimmy Barkenfalt together just bugged me.

Then suddenly I realized what it was. Jimmy Barkenfalt and Grandma didn't match up. Having them together made life seem all kerflooey—like the TV screen when Stephanie messed with the dials.

Anyway, there was nothing I could do about it, was there? They were married, and that was that.

One hundred ninety-eight . . . one hundred ninety-nine . . . *two hundred.*

I let Regina go scratch her kitty condo and shook out my fingers. By now, Daddy was home. When I walked back into the kitchen, he was washing pots, and Mom was in an extreme state of hyper.

"Howdy, Princess," Daddy said. "My hands are soapy, or I'd—"

"That's okay, Daddy." I raised up on tiptoe to kiss his cheek, but Mom stuck a bunch of feathery green leaves between us.

"Deal with this, okay?" she said.

"Uh . . . you mean, wash it and chop it?"

"Well, what *else* do you do with dill? And don't forget to dry it in the spinner before you chop."

She turned her back to switch on the blender, and I nodded and whispered, "Yes, Your Majesty."

Meanwhile, my dad was shouting over the noise, "Anyway, hon, I'm sure you've been a perfect hostess. Not that he sounds like the kind to be picky. Hawaiian shirt and Bermuda shorts, huh? I can't wait to see this guy."

Mom took a deep breath, turned the blender off, and took another deep breath. Then she stuck a spoon in and tasted the soup. "Needs dill," she said. But she smiled at Daddy. "You're right, Don. You're absolutely right. I just need to relax. Relax, relax, re—*oh!*" She jumped. "I didn't see you standing—"

"Didn' mean to startle ya, Lila." Jimmy Barkenfalt was in the kitchen doorway, with Grandma and the nuisance behind him. "Now, don't tell me, Joe. This is your dad, am I right?"

"Dad and bottle-washer, sir. The pleasure's mine." Daddy started to wipe his wet hands on his slacks, but he saw Mom's scowl and grabbed a towel instead. He shook hands with Jimmy Barkenfalt, then held out a hand to Grandma, too. She ignored it and gave him a huge hug.

I had to blink twice. Grandma giving Daddy a hug? I didn't mind exactly. It had just never happened before. I couldn't help but wonder what was coming next. Maybe Grandma would show up for breakfast in bunny slippers.

"Grampa's takin' us out t'dinner!" The nuisance couldn't contain his news.

Grandma looked at Mom. "Now, wait a minute. We said only if it's okay. Looks to me as though your mama has something planned."

"Oh, *please*, Mom? I *can't* eat more o' that French stuff." The nuisance pulled his T-shirt up to display his chubby tummy. "See? I'm *starving*."

Daddy laughed. "I'm sure Lila's dinner will keep. She was just saying that the soup needs time to chill, weren't you, hon?"

"N-no," Mom stammered, "that is, *yes*, but I did have dinner arranged and—"

"Well, that settles it. We'll eat in. Nothin' like home cooking if y'ask me," Jimmy Barkenfalt said. "Don't fret, Joe. We'll go out another night. What's for chow, anyway?"

"Vichyssoise," my mother answered.

The nuisance made a terrible face. Jimmy Barkenfalt gulped. "That's cold soup, isn't it?"

Mom nodded.

"Mmmm-*mm*." Maybe Jimmy Barkenfalt had taken drama classes, too. "Sounds *yummy*. Uh . . . so that's it, then? *Just* cold soup?"

"Oh, no! Two salads. Lentils with oranges and jicama, and arugula with gorgonzola and walnuts."

"*Well*, then," said Jimmy Barkenfalt. "See, Joe? Nothin' to worry about. Y'got your fruit-and-nut salads, not to mention cold soup. Sounds great to me. Who needs meat and potatoes, anyway?" He patted his belly. "I eat too much as it is."

The nuisance was scrunching up his eyes, all pathetic. For a poor, dumb four-year-old, he's smart about crying. He saves it for important stuff. I picked up the twisty and wrapped it around the dill so I could put it back in the fridge. Mom or no Mom, it was obvious how this was going to turn out.

A few minutes later, Jimmy Barkenfalt asked the nuisance where he wanted to go to eat, and my brother got a double bonanza.

"McDonald's," he answered. His cheeks were still tear streaked, and nobody dared contradict him.

"That's my favorite, too!" said Jimmy Barkenfalt.

Mom looked like she had a tummy ache just thinking about it.

Chapter Seven

At dinner, we all had Big Macs, fries, and Cokes, except for Mom. First she said she wasn't hungry, then she changed her mind and had a salad with no dressing and a large chocolate shake.

"Diet special, eh, Lila?" Jimmy Barkenfalt chuckled.

Daddy laughed. Mom smiled a drama-class smile. A little later, when Jimmy Barkenfalt fed my grandmother a couple of his french fries, Mom excused herself to go to the ladies' room. I was getting the idea that Mom felt the same as I did. Maybe she wanted to like Jimmy Barkenfalt, but she just couldn't.

Everybody else was having a great time, though. Daddy and the nuisance and Jimmy Barkenfalt laughed a lot. Daddy asked a lot of questions, and I found out Jimmy Barkenfalt had never even been married before. And he wasn't a doctor or a college professor or even a lawyer. He used to be a tailor. Now he owned a bunch of discount clothing stores.

"Polyester's been very, very good to me," he said. Daddy cracked up.

Jimmy Barkenfalt and my grandmother lived in the same condo complex in Florida. They met in the hallway. She was on her knees, looking for a button that had popped off her sweater, and he found it for her. Then he offered to sew it back on.

"Can you imagine anything so chivalrous?" my grandmother asked. "I never met a man who sewed."

"You might call it love at first stitch!" said Jimmy Barkenfalt.

After we got home, I pulled the big dictionary out of my mom's desk and looked up "chivalrous." It turns out to be a terribly old word for being polite to a woman. I didn't see how sewing buttons exactly qualified.

I was on my way to bed when I heard Mom and Dad having a "lively discussion." They never fight,

Mom claims. But once in a while they do have a lively discussion.

The voices were coming from their bedroom, and I stopped at the closed door to listen. I have to do this. In Stephanie's house, with all the yelling, you can't help but know what everybody's thinking. In my house, you eavesdrop or miss out.

I heard Mom say, "But how can you—"

And Daddy interrupted. "Oh, for heaven's sake, hon. After that stick-in-the-mud, she *deserves* a little fun!"

"Stick-in-the-mud!" Now Mom was too mad to keep her voice down. "He was a *fine, noble*—"

"—fine, noble, *and* a stick-in-the-mud," Dad said firmly. "I always thought it was appropriate that his job was putting people to sleep."

What was a stick-in-the-mud, anyway? Somebody boring, it sounded like. I always thought Daddy liked Grandfather.

My parents were still talking, but I couldn't hear the words any more. There was some stomping around, and then it got quiet.

I didn't sleep very well. Maybe I was upset about Mom and Dad's discussion. Maybe it was too weird to have Grandma and Jimmy Barkenfalt together in the next room. Or maybe there's just too much grease in a Big Mac and fries, which usually Mom never lets us eat.

I was still yawning when I finally came down the back stairs. I could hear Grandma's voice, and when I walked into the kitchen, she was sitting at the breakfast table with Jimmy Barkenfalt. Mom was pouring orange juice.

"You're staying a *week*?" Mom missed the glass and splashed Jimmy Barkenfalt's lap. "Oh, my goodness! I'm so *sorry*. I—"

"Nothin' to worry about. Nothin' at all." Jimmy Barkenfalt popped out of his chair. His shorts were soaked. "One thing about being in the rag trade, I got racks o' clothes, all easy-care polyester!" He kissed my grandmother on the head, and as he passed me to go back upstairs, said, "Good morning, Little Missy."

I watched him go. He was dressed in another Hawaiian outfit, and I couldn't help thinking he looked like a beach ball perched on toothpicks.

"Good morning, dear," Grandma said.

I felt guilty when I looked around, like maybe she had read my mind. "Hi. G'morning," I said. At least she was wearing her usual high heels, not bunny slippers.

Grandma leaned back from the table and looked down at my mom, who was sponging up the juice on the floor. "I thought you'd be pleased we're staying a while, Lila. I want you to get to know Jimmy like I do."

"*As* I do." Mom stood up. "Not *like* I do. For goodness' sake, Mother. Have *all* your standards declined?"

Even I caught her drift. My grandmother's eyes widened, and her perfect posture got even more perfect. I squirmed in my chair.

Mom closed her eyes. "I'm sorry, Mother," she said. "I didn't mean—"

"Oh, but I think you *did* mean," Grandma answered.

Mom started to say something else, but the nuisance came *thwapa-thwapa* down the stairs and ran full speed into the kitchen. He was wearing his Spiderman underwear and nothing else.

Daddy clomped in right behind him. "Come back, you little fugitive!" Daddy grabbed for him, but the nuisance wrapped himself around Grandma's legs.

"Save me!" he yelled.

"Yuk-*o*," I said. His nose was running, and he wiped it on my grandmother's skirt.

I thought she'd have a royal fit, but she laughed. "My handkerchief's upstairs, Joey. Come on, and I'll get you dressed. Maybe we'll even find you a little surprise up there."

"A present? Yay! Gimme!" The nuisance grabbed Grandma's hand and pulled her away from the table.

"Bless you, Grandma," Daddy said. Then he looked around. "What happened to Jimmy B.?"

"He's changing his clothes," I said. "Mom poured orange juice in his lap."

"Honey! You *poured*—"

"Oh, I did not," Mom snapped. "A few drops spilled." She slid three pancakes onto Daddy's plate and glared at me.

I ate my pancakes fast, told my dad I was late, and asked to be excused. I was afraid when everybody else came back, there'd be a lively discussion, or maybe even some stomping around. I didn't want to be there for that.

At the front door, I grabbed my jacket and my backpack and hollered, "Bye, Mom! Bye, Dad! Bye, nuisance! Bye, Grandma! Bye—uh . . . bye. . . ."

I stopped. What was I supposed to call Jimmy Barkenfalt, anyway? The nuisance called him Grandpa, but *no way*.

For a second, I stood there like an idiot. Then I shrugged, swung the door shut, and ran down the front walk. I'd never felt so happy to be out of my own house.

Chapter Eight

A burst of red and yellow leaves blew out of the elm tree in front and—*caaaaw-caaaaw-CAAW*—I heard the crows scolding something. When I looked up, I saw a fat squirrel at the center of the fuss. Every time he chattered, he made the crows holler and the branches shudder.

It was a windy morning, and the fall leaves swirled and crinkled as I walked down the sidewalk. At the corner of Banner Drive, I met up with Sarah J. She's the quiet Sarah in my class. Sarah P. is the noisy one.

Sarah J. is not my good friend because she is so quiet I can hardly hear her when she talks, which she doesn't do much, anyway. But sometimes if you tell her something, she says something pretty intelligent back.

This morning I had a lot to tell her. By the time we got to school, I had described everything about my beautiful grandmother, my stick-in-the-mud grandfather who died, and Jimmy Barkenfalt who knows how to sew on buttons.

"My dad and the nuisance—that's my little brother—think Jimmy Barkenfalt's great. But I dunno. It's like everything in my life has been ker-flooey since I even heard about him." We walked through the door of Room 10 together. "And I don't think my mom likes him, either. Actually, I think she might *hate* him."

"He sounds nice," said Sarah J. It was the first thing she had said, besides hello, all the way to school.

I frowned. I must not have explained it right. "Really?"

She nodded. "Maybe you just have to get used to him."

I was annoyed with Sarah J. She must not be as intelligent as I thought.

I sat down at my desk and got my math home-work out, along with a couple of sharp pencils. Then the bell rang, and a few seconds later Stephanie came loping in. Our teacher, Mrs.

March, folded her arms across her chest and gave her a terribly stern look. Stephanie smiled and said hi, like she had no idea you could get in trouble for being late a thousand zillion mornings in a row.

Actually, Stephanie is in trouble so much, I don't think she knows the difference. I really admire her for this. If I ever got in trouble, I would wilt.

"Please stand for the flag salute." Mrs. March always stands straight as an army sergeant, and she's about the right size for one, too.

When we were all standing, Mrs. March put her hand over her heart, the signal to begin. In front of me, Willie stood on one foot, then the other. His shirt was untucked, and his right shoelace flopped on the floor.

"I pledge allegiance to the flag . . ."

As usual, Sarah P.'s voice rose above everybody else's.

". . . and to the republic, for which it stands . . ."

Next to me, Sierra was moving her lips, but no sound came out. She wears bell-bottoms and tie-dyed shirts and says she doesn't approve of patriotism.

". . . liberty and justice for all."

"Homework, please, ladies and gentlemen." Mrs. March said that like it was part of the flag salute. Liberty, justice, and homework for all.

Sam's hand shot up. "The reason I couldn't do the homework is—"

"No excuses, Samuel. You may stay in at the break and do it," said Mrs. March. "Stephanie? Your homework is . . . ?"

"Didn't feel like doing it," Stephanie said, and before Mrs. March could react, "I know, I know. I'll do it at break."

After the chaos at my house, it felt great to be in Room 10, even if I was annoyed with Sarah J. Everybody was acting just like they were supposed to, like they did every day. It was all terribly comforting and normal.

Since Stephanie had to do math at break, I didn't have a chance to talk to her till lunch. Of course, she was curious about Jimmy Barkenfalt, and when I told her everything, she said he sounded "pukey."

I nodded. "Yeah, *pukey*." I'd never said that word before. At home, a word like that would get me grounded for a thousand zillion lifetimes. I knew because of what had happened the time the nuisance came home from preschool and called me "barf-brain," loud enough for Mom to hear. There was so much stomping and glaring, even he got the idea, and he hasn't said anything like it since.

"Maybe he's not *just* pukey." Stephanie was chewing a tuna sandwich, and I could smell fish even from across the table. "Maybe he's a *bad guy*. Like on *America's Most Wanted*. Your gran's rich, right?"

"I dunno," I said. I felt embarrassed. In my family, we never talk about money. It's supposed to be impolite. But Stephanie is always asking me things like how much a CFO makes. I guess it shouldn't bother me and anyway, I have no idea.

"She *looks* rich," said Stephanie. "And your gramps was a doctor, right? So then she has to be rich. Anyway, I bet this guy married her for her money. Or maybe even to *steal* her money. Remember that movie we watched?"

Movie? For a second, I didn't know what she was talking about. Then I remembered *Night Must Fall*, where the evil strangler wanted to murder the old lady.

"The strangler's name was Jimmy, too." Stephanie raised her eyebrows like this was terribly significant.

I shook my head. "Holy moly, Steph. Get real. Jimmy Barkenfalt might be kind of, well . . . *pukey* . . . but he's not gonna strangle anybody. Anyway, he doesn't even need money. He owns all these stores, like I said."

"You think he's gonna advertise that he's a strangler?" she asked. "Anybody can claim they own stores. How do you know it's true?"

"I know it's true because . . ." I stopped. Come to think of it, I didn't know it was true. But of course it was true.

"Did you ever hear of a store called Barkenfalt's? No way. I bet . . ." Stephanie kept talking, and Jimmy Barkenfalt got worse with every word. He'd probably married other little old ladies and strangled them, too. Dozens of them. Stephanie had heard of guys like that. If we were lucky, maybe the police were onto him. Maybe they'd arrest him at *our* house! They'd bust down the doors with their guns blazing, and we'd all die in the crossfire. . . .

"Steph! For golly sake!" I interrupted. "Real life isn't like that!"

"How do *you* know what real life is like? You don't even watch TV."

Stephanie is my best friend, but when you're arguing with her, she doesn't play fair. "Look," I said finally, "he's just pukey, okay? That's the worst you can say about him."

And after all she'd come up with, pukey didn't sound bad.

Chapter Nine

When I got home from school, there was a note on the kitchen table.

Molly,

Mr. Barkenfalt is taking care of Joe at the park. Grandmother and I have gone to tea downtown. For your snack, I made bran muffins. They're in the tin on the counter.

Home soon.

Mom

I poured myself a glass of milk, got out a muffin, peeled the paper off, and took a bite. Good. No dried cranberries this time.

While I chewed, I thought about the things Stephanie had said at lunch. It was all crazy, wasn't it? I tried to picture what a real strangler would be like. I figured he'd have a stubbly beard and wear dark clothes. Also, it made sense that a strangler would be grumpy. A happy person would have no reason to strangle anybody.

Jimmy Barkenfalt was terribly cheerful, clean shaven, and he always wore colorful clothes. Therefore, Stephanie was wrong. Like I ever doubted it.

I swallowed the last of the muffin and got up to rinse out my glass. Still, Stephanie did have a point. I never watch TV, never even once saw *America's Most Wanted*. Stephanie hardly ever missed it. Didn't that make her a sort of expert on the criminal mind?

Mom's note was still on the table: *Mr. Barkenfalt is taking care of Joe at the park.*

My baby brother. Alone. With Jimmy Barkenfalt. The strangler.

I put my jacket back on. I had math homework and a spelling test the next day, but they could wait a few minutes. Of course, I knew I was being crazy. But it wouldn't hurt to make sure.

The park is only a block away from my house. When I first pushed open the gate by the soccer field, I didn't see anybody at all.

As I walked across the field toward the playground, I saw some big kid on top of the slide, waving like an idiot. Don't you just hate it when big kids take over the equipment so little kids are scared to use it? And this one was fat, too. But where was the nuisance? And Jimmy Barkenfalt?

To tell you the truth, I was getting worried. It was pathetic, but I had let Stephanie get to me. I started to run, and a second later I realized it wasn't a big kid on the slide at all. It was Jimmy Barkenfalt. If he'd been wearing his usual beach-ball clothes, I would have recognized him faster. But now he had on a dark gray shirt and black pants.

Holy moly. This was too weird. This was almost *scary*. A grown man, a grown man married to my grandmother, on top of the kiddie slide, acting crazy. And what had he done with my brother?

I stopped to look around. My eyes darted everywhere, but I didn't see the nuisance . . . or did I? Wait a minute. Someone was sitting on the bench by the jungle gym. He was the right size to be the nuisance, but he looked all wrong. Were those glasses he was wearing? And what was that around his neck—a tie? There was something in his lap, too. A *newspaper*?

"Look at me! Look at me!" Now Jimmy Barkenfalt

was not only waving, he was yelling. The next thing I knew, he had sat himself down, and then he was sliding, and then—*ooooff*—he landed on his bottom in the sand.

I ran the rest of the way to the bench. "*Joey*, is that *you*?" I panted. "Are you okay?"

The nuisance pushed the glasses back on his nose and shook the newspaper. "Careful there, son," he said in a deep voice. "Would you like me to push you on the swings now?"

Huh?

"Oh, hi, Molly." The nuisance smiled up at me. "I mean, *Hello, Little Missy*." Then he whispered. "I'm pretending I'm Grandpa, and he's pretending he's me. See? It was his idea."

Jimmy Barkenfalt stumbled to his feet, ran over to us, and jumped up and down a couple of times, like a little kid who has to go to the bathroom. "Hi, Molly! We're gonna go on the swings now, wanna come? Huh? Huh? Huh?"

This had to be the goofiest thing I ever heard of, but I was so relieved, I laughed. And anyway, it was sort of funny. The nuisance was laughing so hard he had to hold his tummy.

"Sure, I'll come," I said. "But I've got homework, you know. Not to mention Regina. The Cool-Cat Cat Show—"

"—is on Sunday, we *know,*" the nuisance said. "Don't worry, Little Missy." He patted my hand. "We'll get you home in time."

In his dark pants and shirt, Jimmy Barkenfalt looked a little less ridiculous than usual. I don't mean he looked handsome or anything. Just more like a regular, serious grown-up. He must have noticed me looking at his clothes because he said, "Too cold for shorts. But these dark colors are as gloomy as the weather, am I right? I feel like a hangman or somethin'. The tie was s'posed to liven things up, but I went and lent it to Gramps here."

He nodded at the nuisance, who was running ahead of us toward the swings, practically tripping over the orange-and-yellow tie. I wished Jimmy Barkenfalt hadn't gone and said "hangman." Along with the tie around my brother's neck, it made me remember my theory that stranglers wear dark clothes.

Without turning my head, I looked sideways to see if there was stubble on Jimmy Barkenfalt's jaw. Nope. So that meant . . .

Molly, get a grip, I lectured myself. What that meant was: Exactly nothing. The whole thing was ridiculous. I didn't know anything about stranglers and anyway, Jimmy Barkenfalt wasn't one.

"Hard work entertaining these little kids," he whispered to me as we came up to the swings.

"What kind o' homework you got, anyway? I used to be pretty good at math."

"Oh . . . uh, thanks, but I'm supposed to do it by myself," I said.

He settled his bottom into a swing. "Suit yourself," he said, then, in a little-kid voice, he whined, "Gramps, gimme a push, okay? Plee-ee-ee-ze? Plee-ee-ee-ze?"

The nuisance backed up so he could get a running start, closed his eyes, put his arms out in front of him, and charged full speed at Jimmy Barkenfalt's huge body. Even with all that work, he only shoved the swing forward about a foot. And then he couldn't back out of the way in time; he just kept going forward.

Blam-o! Jimmy Barkenfalt swung back, and the nuisance got clobbered.

"Weeee-aaaa-aaaa-aah!" the poor nuisance howled from where he lay on the ground.

"Joey, where'd he get ya? What hurts?" I knelt next to him. Then I looked Jimmy Barkenfalt right in the eyes. "You knocked him down!"

Jimmy Barkenfalt didn't blink. "Guilty as charged," he said. "Let's have a look, son. Are ya bleedin' anywheres?"

The nuisance was crying too hard to answer. Poor, dumb four-year-old. He's pretty heavy, but I figured if I could balance him over one shoulder I could get him home. I was going to pick him up, but Jimmy Barkenfalt beat me to it. "Here, Joe, grab on to my neck, there. We'll take you back, have a look at your injuries." He heaved my soggy brother up, then jerked to his feet, cringing and grunting. "*Ooooof*—sacroiliac ain't what she used to be. There, Joey. How you doin'? Better?"

The nuisance's sobs had turned into stuttering breaths. Even so, I didn't like the idea of Jimmy Barkenfalt with his arms around *my* brother. "You sure you're okay, Joe?" I asked. "I could carry you. Are you *sure*—"

"I'b okay," he sniffled. "Grandpa's got me."

Jimmy Barkenfalt patted his back. "'At's right, Joey. No sweat." The two of them started across the soccer field, with me tagging along like some stranger. Every few steps I asked the nuisance if he was sure he was okay, and every few steps he nodded and sniffled and wiped his nose on Jimmy Barkenfalt's orange-and-yellow tie. Yuk-*o*.

Mom and Grandma weren't home when we got there. So Jimmy Barkenfalt had to wash Joe's face and look him over for blood. There wasn't any. I have to admit Jimmy Barkenfalt did a pretty good job with the first-aid stuff, and he never once got grumpy about the snail trail of snot on his tie.

Chapter Ten

Tea did not improve things between Mom and Grandma.

And neither did vichyssoise, which we finally ate for dinner that night. At the table, Jimmy Barkenfalt told how he used to love leftover mashed potatoes when he was a kid. He was trying to say something nice, I think, but Mom didn't appreciate having her gourmet soup compared to leftover mashed potatoes.

Not even Daddy could make things better. He started to tell about his day—something to do with immortalizing goodwill, I think. I didn't understand a word, but Jimmy Barkenfalt asked a couple of questions. Mom wasn't even listening.

She kept making dagger eyes at Grandma, and Grandma kept looking over everybody's head instead of into their faces.

Finally, Daddy gave up and devoted himself to the lentils and the arugula on his plate, even though I happen to know he hates them both.

Only the nuisance was happy. Mom served fig mousse for dessert, and there was lots of whipped cream on it. He and Jimmy Barkenfalt were sitting next to each other, and they sculpted faces in the whipped cream until they realized both Mom and Grandma were staring.

I wouldn't have thought things could get worse, but they did because Grandma picked that moment to spring the huge surprise: They were taking us all to DizzyPark Sunday.

Sunday, get it? The day of the Cool-Cat Cat Show. And it couldn't be any other day because they had discount coupons. So guess who had to miss out?

"Too bad, Molly," said the nuisance. He didn't mean it one bit.

When Mom volunteered to skip DizzyPark and take me to the Cool-Cat Cat Show, Jimmy Barkenfalt said, "Oh, that's a shame, Lila." But Grandma didn't argue.

As soon as the plates were cleared, Daddy disappeared into the basement to work on his stamps.

Mom did the dishes, and Grandma went upstairs to read to the nuisance. One thing about having her and Jimmy Barkenfalt around, the nuisance wasn't nearly as pesty to me as usual.

Actually, I sort of missed him.

I hadn't had time to groom Regina yet, but I also wanted to call Stephanie. Maybe she did think Jimmy Barkenfalt was a strangler, but she was also the only person who would understand how kerflooey my life felt. I mean, since Jimmy Barkenfalt, my family couldn't even eat dinner together.

I went up to my room for some privacy, picked up the phone on my night table, and stopped. Whose voices were those? I didn't mean to listen, but for a second I was so surprised I did anyway.

". . . more headaches over that South American supplier! Well, they can keep their stupid laws; I want that drop-shipped *yesterday,* capeesh?" said one voice.

"I hear ya, J. B. Settle down," somebody else said. "Nothin' I can do about the customs boys, is there?"

"I got too much *couth* t'tell ya whatcha *can* do with 'em. . . ."

That one was Jimmy Barkenfalt's voice, only I'd never heard him like this before. So *grumpy.*

"Aw*right*, aw*right* . . . ," he went on. "Listen up. You tell Manuel he better get back to me pronto if he wants to keep his fanny in one piece. I got no time for—hello? Somebody listenin' in, here?"

I hung up quick. My heart was racing, and I could hardly swallow, my mouth was so dry. He couldn't possibly know it was me on the other phone, could he? And what did all that stuff mean?

Supplier in South America? Stupid laws? Fanny in one piece?

Now I for sure needed to talk to Stephanie. Probably it'd take somebody who watched *America's Most Wanted* every week to translate what Jimmy Barkenfalt was talking about.

A few minutes later, I heard Jimmy Barkenfalt and Grandma in the hallway, so I tried calling Stephanie again. When I explained what I'd heard, she didn't hesitate: "He's a drug lord." She said this the same way you'd say, "He's a dentist."

"What do you mean 'drug lord?' Is that the same as a pusher?"

"*Way* worse. The drug lord's like the boss. Pushers work for him."

I couldn't help remembering that a few hours ago Stephanie had told me Jimmy Barkenfalt was a strangler. "How can you tell?" I asked her.

"Gosh, Molly. If I didn't know you were smart, I'd sure think you were dumb. He said South America, didn't he? That's where they grow drug plants. And that part about 'the customs boys?' They're the police that work at the border, keeping drugs out."

I had to admit she had learned a lot from TV.

"One good thing, though," she added. "Drug lords have a lot of money. So he probably doesn't need to strangle your grandmother. Of course, the FBI might break into your house one night and blast you while you sleep. That happens a lot."

"But what do I do?" I asked. "My grandma's *married* to him! I can't let her be married to a drug lord! What if the police shoot her, too?"

"Hmmmm." She was nodding, I could tell. "I see your point. . . . Hey, I know."

"What?"

"Doesn't your mom have some humongous knives for all her cooking? Maybe you could sneak into the guest room, and—"

"Holy *moly*, Steph! Are you crazy?"

"You're right," she said. "Too messy. Well, doesn't your dad have a gun? Or . . . hey, what about poison? With your mom's food, he'd never know the—"

"Forget it, Steph! I'm not killing anybody."

"Well, if you're going to be a *wimp* about it . . ."

Like I said, Steph doesn't play fair when you argue with her. She didn't really expect me to kill Jimmy Barkenfalt. She just goes for extreme drama. Now I could hear yelling in the background on her end.

"What's going on *there*?" I asked.

"Jerry just came to the door. You know, to pick up Emily. You should see 'im, Molly. He's wearing all black leather, except for a white skull and crossbones on the back of his jacket. He looks *wicked*."

By wicked, I think she meant good. "So Mom's mad as heck, wants him to get the Sam Hill out the door and don't come back, and Emily's crying . . . and, anyway, I can hardly hear you. Tell me at school tomorrow what you decide, okay?"

"What I decide?"

"Yeah, you know. Guns or poison. Anyway, see ya. . . ."

Chapter Eleven

"Ninety-one . . . ninety-two . . . ninety-three . . ."

I had plenty to think about while I brushed Regina that night. If Jimmy Barkenfalt was a drug lord, he was dangerous. So shouldn't I tell the police? But what would I tell them? I had a feeling the story might not sound very convincing to a police officer.

"One hundred twenty-two . . . one hundred twenty-three . . . one hundred twenty-four . . ."

I considered telling Grandma. I considered telling my parents. But if there's one thing I've learned in all my ten years of life, it's that grown-ups stick together. The first thing any of them would do is come right out and ask Jimmy Barkenfalt.

I could just picture my dad: "So, Jimmy B., my daughter, here, says you're really a drug lord. Any truth to that?"

Holy moly.

"One hundred ninety-nine . . . *two hundred.* Okay, Your Long-tailed Highness, time for the comb." I combed her fur in layers, just like the book says to do, and finally let her go. She leaped to the kitty condo and started grooming herself with her tongue, like I hadn't done a good enough job.

With all the chaos over Jimmy Barkenfalt, I guess I wasn't concentrating on the Cool-Cat Cat Show, now only three days away. But most of the work would come Saturday—shampoo, humectant, blow-dry, teeth, ears, claws. Sunday morning at the arena I'd brush her again, then chalk under her tail, under her eyes, and around her paws so they were as white as the rest of her.

It was all planned out, but still I had a worried feeling. Everything else had gone kerflooey; it only made sense that our blue ribbon would, too.

By the time I got upstairs it was almost ten o'clock, and the house was quiet. Usually my parents stayed downstairs watching movies or reading till at least eleven. But having Grandma and Jimmy Barkenfalt around seemed to tire them both out.

I went upstairs, flipped the light switch in my room, and opened my top drawer to get pajamas. That's when, behind me, I heard something rustle. I froze. All my thoughts about criminals and police and guns had me hyper. And now . . . what was this? I turned my head slowly and saw there was something moving in my bed.

"Wha—!" I jumped.

The nuisance, all snuggled up in my covers, put his hand over his eyes and rolled toward me. "Ah uhz oh-nee," he mumbled.

"You were what?"

He yawned. "Oh-nee."

"Oh, *lonely*. Well, y'want me to go get Regina? She'll sleep with you."

He shook his head and rolled away from the light. "Comfy," he said. "Ni-night."

"Wait a minute! You can't stay here!" I put my hand on his shoulder to shake him, but he twitched it off like a horse does a fly.

I know sometimes the nuisance crawls into bed with Mom and Dad, like if he has a bad dream or something. But he'd never come into my room before. Maybe his life felt kerflooey, too. He was having a great time with Jimmy Barkenfalt, but even a four-year-old could probably tell how unhappy Mom was.

I didn't have the heart to move him. So I put on my pajamas and slid into bed. I'd been planning to study for my spelling test first, but the light might bother him. It probably wouldn't matter. The words were easy this week.

No surprise that I didn't sleep, though. Besides thinking every creak was an FBI invasion, I had the nuisance to contend with. He's a small person, but he flopped and punched and kicked so much, he took up the whole bed. It was like being on the edge of a cliff while somebody tried to shove me off.

Of course, *he* never woke up once.

After a night like that, I was grateful when the sun came through my curtains and the first footsteps padded down the hallway.

Then I heard the scream.

Holy moly! The FBI! Stephanie was right! I jumped up and was halfway to my door when I remembered you're supposed to hit the deck when shots are fired. Not that I'd heard shots yet—just yelling.

"Wha'? Hi, Molly." The nuisance sat up in bed.

"Stay *down*!" I jumped flat on top of him.

"*Ow!* Get offa me! Hey—"

"My baby!" It was Mom doing most of the yelling. "Where is he?"

If I hadn't been so sleepy, I would have figured it out faster. Of course it wasn't the FBI at all. It was just Mom, who had gone into the nuisance's room to wake him, seen he wasn't in bed, and freaked out.

By the time my poor sleepy brain put this together, the whole house was awake: Jimmy Barkenfalt had gone running out barefoot into the cold yelling, "Joey! Come back, son! Come to Grandpa!" Grandma was dialing the police. Daddy was saying to hysterical Mom, "Now, we just have to be logical. He's only four. We're smarter than he is."

"He's in here! He's fine. He just—" I hollered. And in about a second everybody was trooping into my room and hugging and kissing the nuisance like he'd just escaped from pirates.

Chapter Twelve

There was a truce at breakfast. The grown-ups were so relieved about Joe that Mom and Grandma even laughed together. Not a drop of orange juice spilled. And back to his beach-ball clothes, Jimmy Barkenfalt looked so silly it was tough for me to imagine him being a drug lord.

The crows were scolding something as I walked out the front door, but this time I didn't see any squirrel. I almost felt like they were scolding *me*. I walked fast, with my feet crunching and scattering dry leaves. If I hurried, I wouldn't run into that annoying Sarah J.

When I got to my desk, I had a few minutes to read over the spelling words. It was warm inside, and immediately I felt sleepy again. The words didn't look so easy now. I remember Daddy told us once about truckers who drive all night. After a while, they see hallucinations, which is like having a dream when you're awake.

I think that's what happened to me later during the test. I looked down at my notebook; the letters swam around like goldfish in a bowl; the paper morphed into a pillow and . . . *thump. Ow!* My head dropped. Willie looked around when he heard the noise and laughed at me, even though when it comes to spelling tests, Willie has nothing to laugh about.

"Are you okay, Molly?" Sierra whispered. "You look kind of . . . uh, *gross.*"

"Thank you," I whispered through a yawn. "I feel gross, too."

"Sierra?" Mrs. March folded her arms across her chest. "Any more talking, and I shall have to confiscate your test."

Sierra shot me a look like, How come she's not yelling at you? And in the back of the class, somebody hummed the first few notes of the death march. "Dum-dum-de-dum . . ." I knew it was Stephanie. You could almost see Mrs. March's blood pressure rise, but nobody giggled and gave Steph away. So all Mrs. March could do was spit out the next word: "Prejudice, as in 'It is wrong to feel prejudice.' "

I scribbled something that started with a *p* and had a *g* in it, and wasn't there a *c* somewhere? I had a very bad feeling about this test.

At lunch, Stephanie sat down next to me in the caf. "Well?"

"Well, what?"

"Gun, knife, or poison?"

"Ha, ha." I leaned my head on one hand and tried to unzip my sandwich bag with the other.

"Actually, you're right. Killing him probably isn't such a hot idea. If you did, his *henchmen* would come after you—*blam-o*!" She made a gun with her fingers and pointed it at my head.

I was still struggling with my sandwich bag. Stephanie must have gotten tired of watching because she took it away, got the sandwich out, and set it on a napkin in front of me.

"Pesto again?" she said.

I sniffed. "Yeah. With feta cheese, smells like. Thanks."

"What's the matter with you, anyway?"

I set down my sandwich, which all of a sudden didn't look that appetizing, and told her about my long night with the nuisance and how I almost fell asleep during the test.

"You have to do something about this Barkenfalt guy," she said. "You can't eat. You can't sleep. You can't spell. He's ruining your life."

Stephanie finished eating and punched her lunchbag into a ball. The lunch aide was looking the other way, and Stephanie tossed the bag over her head and into the trash can. "Two points!" she said. The lunch aide spun around and scowled, but she couldn't tell for sure who threw the bag, so for the second time in one day, Stephanie didn't get in trouble.

"What if your gran decided to divorce him?" she asked.

"But she *loves* him! You should see the way she looks at his bald head."

"What if she thought he was ridiculous, same as you think he is?" Stephanie asked.

"Come on," I said. "Let's go play dodgeball or something." We got up and headed for the exit. "The whole trouble is Grandma *doesn't* think he's ridiculous." I dropped my lunchbag into the trash and smiled at the lunch aide.

"You're such a *wimp,*" Stephanie said as we pushed the caf door open. "Here's a chance to use that brain of yours for something better than school, and you won't do it. If you thought about it, you'd find a way to make him look so ridiculous, even Gran would notice."

Now I was annoyed with Stephanie, or maybe with myself. The dodgeball game was on the lower playground. We sprinted down, and I yelled over to Sam, "Can we play?"

"Time out!" Sam hollered. "Over there." He pointed, and we trotted across the circle. "Yeah, that's good. Okay, time in!"

Sarah P. wasted no time throwing the ball at Stephanie, but Stephanie was just as quick to catch it.

"Ha!" she said and pointed at Sarah P. "You're out!"

Before Steph took her turn, she looked at me. "I don't think you're trying hard enough, Molly. I think if you really wanted to, you could fix that ol' Barkenfalt guy. But good."

Then she threw the ball hard. I tried to dodge right, but it came at me fast and caught my knee. *Blam-o*—I was out.

After lunch, we traded spelling tests to correct them. When Sarah J. handed me back mine, I thought she had made a mistake. There were check marks all over it—*six wrong*! Even Willie had missed only five. Mom knows spelling tests are Friday, so there would be no point trying to hide it from her.

Holy moly. When I got home, I was going to be in extreme trouble.

Chapter Thirteen

By now you know how hyper Mom gets. Well, multiply that about a thousand zillion times and you have what happened after she saw my spelling test. Her voice got very quiet, and she told me this kind of score would never get me into Yale, and didn't I know what the family expected of me? And people who can't spell never appear educated, no matter what else they do.

Then she glared at me and stomped upstairs, but it wasn't long till she stomped back down and started in on me again.

I felt terrible. I wished I was like Stephanie, used to being in trouble so I didn't care. But I hate having anybody mad at me. It makes me feel all withered, like the old dead leaves on the sidewalk.

So even though some part of me knew that not one person at Yale would ever know about this spelling test, I didn't argue. I just ate my day-old bran muffin and drank my milk and felt dried up in silence.

Grandma and Jimmy Barkenfalt had gone shopping, but the nuisance was there for all of it. He had never seen me in trouble before. I could tell by the way he kept looking at Mom that it scared him.

No way was I dumb enough to interrupt Mom. But when she finally stopped, I had a problem. I wanted to brush Regina, but I was afraid Mom might think I was spending too much time on my cat and not enough on my spelling. What if she was so mad, she wouldn't take me to the Cool-Cat Cat Show?

Finally, I got a genius idea: I told her I was going upstairs to study next week's spelling words. My plan was really to do that for a few minutes, then come down and take care of Regina. But when I got to my room and opened the book, the letters did the goldfish thing. I must have fallen asleep in about a half second, because it seemed like right away Mom was calling me.

"Is Joe in your room again?"

I shook my brain awake and looked over on the bed. No nuisance.

"Keep calm, keep calm," Mom was muttering when I came downstairs. "He wasn't gone this morning, so he isn't gone now."

With months of experience finding my cat, I had developed this sort of instinct about searching for hidden creatures. Last time I saw the nuisance, he was in the kitchen. Where would be a good hiding place for somebody his size?

Easy. Sure enough, when I knelt down and opened the Tupperware cupboard, there he was— curled up behind the drainpipes, with Regina and the plastic tubs and the plastic lids and the wadded-up grocery bags.

"What are you doing in there?" I asked.

"Is she gone?"

"Mommy, you mean?"

"I was afraid she might get mad at me, too."

Poor, dumb four-year-old. "She won't get mad at you—at least, not like that. Not till you start taking spelling tests."

"When's that?"

"Second grade. You've got three years."

A few seconds passed while his puny little brain calculated. "Does three years come after Christmas?"

When I nodded, he slithered around the pipes and crawled out. Regina followed him in two quick leaps. "Don't tell Mommy where I was." He bumped the cupboard door shut with his knee. "I might need to hide there again in second grade."

"Oh, thank goodness!" Mom came through the dining-room door. "Where were you?" She bent down and cuddled the nuisance next to her.

The nuisance shut his lips tight.

She looked at me. "Where was he?"

"Uh . . . he just sort of appeared."

"Joe? What in the world?" She pushed him back a little so she could look at him. He kept his mouth shut, and her face did one of its quick changes—from relieved to mad. *"Fine,"* she said. "That's *fine*. One child is failing fifth grade, and the other one won't talk."

The nuisance gave me a look that said, Didn't you just promise she wouldn't get mad at me till second grade? I thought he'd start crying; that's what I would've done. But he didn't. He turned back to Mom and glared a sort of four-year-old glare. "You're a barf-brain!" he said.

I don't think I've ever been that surprised. I know there are plenty of other little kids who say worse stuff to their parents, but never in our family.

Mom was speechless for a second, and then something just terrible happened. She raised her hand up and swung it around—*slap!*—against my little brother's bottom. The sound seemed to echo around the kitchen.

I don't have to tell you the nuisance had never been spanked before. There was another stunned moment, then his little face puckered up all the way from his hair to his chin. Now he was going to cry for real.

"Oh my . . ." Mom looked at the hand that had slapped Joe, like she didn't recognize it. He was wailing by now, but instead of picking him up or hugging him or saying she was sorry or *anything*, she knelt there frozen on the kitchen floor.

"Come on, nuisance," I said. "Let's go take care of Regina, okay? You can help."

Ignoring Mom, I picked him up and sort of half dragged, half carried him to Regina's room. Then I set him down on the grooming table. He was still crying.

I thought of going back to see if Mom was okay, or if she was still stuck on the floor, staring at her hand. But I didn't. The nuisance was right: She was a barf-brain.

Chapter Fourteen

"Seventeen . . . eighteen . . . twenty-five . . . fifty-'leven . . . a hundred . . ."

Brushing Regina made the nuisance feel better, same as it usually makes me feel better. He had gone from crying to whimpering, then from whimpering to sniffling. By now he was normal, except his face was pink, with yuk-o streaks of tears and snot. I was hoping his hand would get tired soon because, to tell you the truth, every time he brushed, he tangled a new tangle.

"Seven . . . eight . . . forty-six . . . forty-eight . . . twenty-fifty . . ."

suddenly Daddy was standing in Regina's room, still holding his briefcase. Before I could answer, he noticed the nuisance's face. "Joey, are you okay?"

"Uh-huh. Fine. Oh, 'cept for Mommy hit me."

"*What?*" He looked at the nuisance, then at me. "Molly . . . ?"

"Yeah, it's true," I said. "She did."

"But why . . . ? Where . . . ?"

"On my butt. Wanna see?" The nuisance dropped the kitty brush. Then, just as quickly, he dropped his pants and mooned us.

Usually, Daddy would have laughed. Even I might have. But this was too weird. "Uh . . . that'll do, thanks, Joe," Daddy said. "You look . . . uh, fine, I guess. Molly?"

"Yeah. His bottom's good."

"No, no. What I meant was, what happened? We don't spank you children. I can't even imagine . . ." His voice sort of faded away.

I didn't know how to answer. I mean, I could tell Daddy that Mom slapped Joe because Joe called her a barf-brain. But I knew that wasn't the whole reason. It was also that Joe had been hiding, plus there was my spelling test, plus Joe wasn't in his bed this morning. . . .

And before that there was the fight between her and Grandma.

I thought back and back and back, trying to get to the real reason Mom had slapped the nuisance. Then it hit me. The trouble wasn't really that Mom was a barf-brain. The trouble was her life; it was in an extreme state of kerflooey, just like mine.

And why was it kerflooey?

"Jimmy Barkenfalt." I said it out loud, even though I didn't mean to.

"What? Jimmy Barkenfalt?" Now Daddy was really confused.

"No, Molly." The nuisance shook his head. "Grandpa didn't hit me. *Mommy* hit me."

"Glad we have that settled." Mom came up behind Daddy. I wondered if she'd been sitting on the kitchen floor the whole time.

Daddy set down his briefcase and looked at her. "Hon? *Honey?* What happened?"

She put her palm on her forehead and closed her eyes. "I think I need to lie down," she said.

"Mommy?" The nuisance said it in this sad little voice. I knew just how he felt because even though I'm ten and way too old for that stuff, I felt sad, too.

That's when Mom melted. She dropped her hand, looked from him to me, and then her face puckered up. *Holy moly,* I thought.

Chapter Fifteen

So after all the terrible stuff, one good thing happened. Mom practically squished the nuisance and me with this huge, tearful hug. And then Daddy joined in and hugged everybody, even Her Long-tailed Highness.

I was trying to breathe and wondering if now we'd be a huggy family like Stephanie's, when I heard Grandma and Jimmy Barkenfalt come in the front door. We all let go of each other, and for one happy second I liked my whole family and maybe the whole world.

Then Jimmy Barkenfalt charged in. "What's for chow? I'm starved!" he announced.

Regina was trying to claw any exposed human

flesh because she had been at the core of the huge hug and didn't like it a bit. At the sound of Jimmy Barkenfalt's voice, she finally tore loose and sprinted for the doorway.

"Hey, furball—" Jimmy Barkenfalt reached for her, but she brushed his leg and got past. *"Aaaaaaah-choo!"* He sneezed loudly, then pulled a pink polka-dot handkerchief out of his pocket and blew his nose. "Sorry," he sniffled. "I've been allergic to furballs since I was a little shaver." He snorted and sniffled a couple more times, then he wadded up the handkerchief and crammed it back into his pocket.

Yuk-*o*. Even Grandma looked annoyed. And I was for sure done with liking everybody.

As you could probably figure out, Mom had been too busy to make dinner. First she had to do all that stomping and glaring over my spelling test. Then, I guess, she had to stare at her hand. Anyway, since she is not the kind who will open a package of ramen noodles, there had to be a huge discussion of what to eat.

Of course, the nuisance was all for McDonald's again, but then Daddy suggested the grown-ups go someplace fancy Mom would like. He was trying to calm her down, I could tell. The nuisance and I would have pizza here with Dena Dooley, our usual baby-sitter.

An hour later, the grown-ups were gone; the pizza was gone; Dena Dooley was talking on the phone; the nuisance was watching one of Mom's movies; and I was brushing Regina—trying to undo the damage the nuisance did before.

"Forty-seven . . . forty-eight . . . forty-nine . . ."

After a day full of stuff to think about, one thing kept bugging me: My best friend had called me a wimp. And she had said something else, too. . . . Oh yeah— "If you thought about it, you'd find a way to make Jimmy Barkenfalt look so ridiculous, even Gran would notice."

And if I could make Grandma think he was ridiculous, then would she leave him?

But it didn't matter because it was impossible. I mean, without my doing anything, Jimmy Barkenfalt was as ridiculous as it is possible for one man to be. And still Grandma gave him these adoring looks. There was only one time when she seemed to notice how yuk-o he really is—before they left for dinner, when Regina made him sneeze and snort.

"One hundred twenty-six . . . one hundred twenty-seven . . . one hundred twenty-eight . . ."

And that's when I got this idea.

"But it'd never work," I told Regina. Then I said it two more times, trying to convince myself. But I didn't convince myself. Because—unfortunately— it was a very good idea.

Grandma was usually a smart person. This Jimmy Barkenfalt thing was just a goof in her usually perfect life. All she needed was a nudge, and she was bound to see Jimmy Barkenfalt the same way Mom and I did. After that, she'd realize she'd made a terrible mistake.

My idea was the perfect nudge.

I brushed a few more strokes—I was so hyper by now that I'd lost count—and then I got the comb. I had to bend down to get at a tangle, and Regina flicked her tail in my face.

"I know this is the perfect time, while they're out to dinner. I know I ought to do it right now. This very minute. But . . ." I tried to think of an excuse.

I tried harder.

Regina had been sitting on her grooming table, eyeing me, but now she jumped to her condo and ripped into it. I combed a ball of fluffy white fur out of the kitty brush. But this time, instead of throwing the fur in the wastebasket, I got a plastic bag and zipped it inside.

That white fluff was my ammo.

Chapter Sixteen

Dena Dooley was pacing back and forth in the kitchen when I walked by. She had her shoulder hunched next to her ear to keep the phone in place, and while she talked, she spooned banana-praline sorbet from the carton into her mouth.

". . . so *she* said, y'know, Trevor is like *so* immature, but if she doesn't go with him, maybe she won't, y'know, like have a date at *all.* Then *Spencer* said . . ."

I shook my head. Yuk-o. I swear, I'm *never* going to be a teenager.

It was 8:00 by the kitchen clock, and I wasn't sure what time the grown-ups would be home. I really wanted to call Stephanie. I knew she'd never let me wimp out. But if I said I needed the phone, Dena would just smile and nod and wave me off.

But at least with Dena busy yakking, I could be sure she wouldn't interfere with my plan.

Next, I looked in the family room, where the nuisance was in an extreme state of zombie in front of the TV. He wouldn't bother me, either.

Halfway up the stairs, I realized I was walking on tiptoe. I knew there was no one on the landing, but even so, I looked right and left when I got there. Then I started tiptoeing again. I could feel my heart—*thud-thud-thud*—when I pushed the guest-room door open. *Cree-e-e-eak* went the hinges, and I jumped like I'd seen toes poking out from under the bed.

"Calm down," I whispered to myself, and I took a deep breath. The room had a strange, medicine-perfume smell—like shaving cream mixed with deodorant mixed with mouthwash. On the dresser were two suitcases. One was open, with clothes neatly folded inside. The other was half shut, with wads of clothes stuffed inside and on top.

You can figure out which was whose.

Now that I was in here, I wished I had time to snoop. Who knows what clue to Jimmy Barkenfalt's secret life might be lying around? Maybe drugs? Not that I have any idea what drugs look like.

Anyway, if my plan worked, it wouldn't matter. Jimmy Barkenfalt would be out of my life forever.

The bedspread was turned down. That should have made it easy. It wasn't till I sat on the bed that I realized I had a problem. A huge problem: Which side did Jimmy Barkenfalt sleep on?

I stared at the two white pillows but that didn't tell me anything. Then I had an idea. It seemed sort of creepy, like poking around in somebody's underwear drawer. But it was the only idea I had.

So I picked up the nearest pillow, put it against my nose, and sniffed.

Hairspray? Maybe. But it could be aftershave, too. I sniffed the other one. Same thing. *Holy moly.* My grandmother and Jimmy Barkenfalt even smelled alike!

Now I was getting desperate. The alarm clock on the bedside table said 8:18. How long did it take to eat dinner at a fancy place? The clock clicked to 8:19, and that's when I noticed something. On the table next to the clock was a book called *Rebecca,* written by Daphne Something-I-couldn't-pronounce. I checked the table on the other side. A magazine lay open on top of it. I crawled across the bed and closed it so I could read the cover: *Polyester Today.*

Mystery solved! It didn't take an IQ of a thousand zillion to figure out who was reading what.

So this was it. The moment I had waited for. Time to execute my plan.

A second passed. Then a couple more. I didn't move. I just sat there. Wasn't it a really mean thing I was going to do? Make a person sick on purpose? Make him so snotty and sneezy that even his new wife would think he was yuk-o?

"But he's a drug lord," I reminded myself. "At least, I think he is. And he's made my life kerflooey, our whole family's life. . . ."

That did it. I unzipped the plastic bag, took out the ball of cat fur, and stuffed it into Jimmy Barkenfalt's pillowcase.

I was plumping up the pillow when I heard the front door open. *Holy moly! They were home!*

I bounced off the bed. But when I took a last look back, I saw the pillow was all lumpy where the cat fur was.

How fast could Jimmy Barkenfalt and my grandmother come up the stairs, anyway? They were pretty old.

I turned around, reached into the pillowcase and sort of smoothed the fur around. Then I admired my work. A nice, plump, booby-trapped pillow. He would never suspect a thing. I was tip-toeing toward the door when I heard *cree-e-e-e-eak*. Next thing I knew, the door swung wide open.

And there stood Jimmy Barkenfalt.

Chapter Seventeen

For one really terrible second, I thought I was going to wet my pants. Till now I'd only worried about getting in normal trouble. Face to face with Jimmy Barkenfalt, I had a way worse thought. What if he really was a drug lord? What if he knew I knew? What if he thought I was spying for the FBI?

Probably there was a gun scrunched in with the wadded-up clothes in his suitcase. . . . *Blam-o!*

I felt the blood drain out of my face. Why, oh why, hadn't I just stayed a wimp?

"Oh—excuse me, Little Missy," Jimmy Barkenfalt said. "Were you . . . uh . . . looking for something?"

He looked almost as surprised as I was terrified. But he did have a smile on his face. Was it for real? Or was he trying to fool me into not running away?

I gulped and opened my mouth and closed it again. For the first time in all my ten years of life, I knew what that expression "heart in your throat" means. Only it was more like a bowling ball in my throat.

"What's the matter? Furball got your tongue?" Jimmy Barkenfalt laughed. "Hey, that's a good one, am I right?"

I nodded and swallowed again. The bowling ball shrank enough that I could choke out a few words. "I was looking for something." Then I had a bright idea. "For my furball—I mean my cat."

"Ain't seen 'er. And I hope she didn't nap in here, neither. I'm allergic, remember?"

"Oh, yeah." I tried to say it all casual, which is not easy when you sound like a frog. "Well, guess I'll try the bathroom."

He didn't move, and I couldn't get out with his beach-ball body in the doorway. Was he trying to trap me?

"Your throat okay, Molly? Ya look pale, too. Coming down with something?" Jimmy Barkenfalt reached toward me, and I stepped back. His hand was big and hairy.

"Sorry." He frowned. "Just wonderin' if you have a fever is all."

I shook my head. "I'm fine." I cleared my throat. "Uh . . . guess I'll look for Regina now."

"Sure." He nodded, but he still didn't move. He definitely suspected something.

Thud-thud-thud—my heart pounded so loud, he could probably hear it. Any second, I was gonna faint.

". . . DizzyPark trip, Missy." Jimmy Barkenfalt was talking, but my imagination had gone so hyper it took a minute for the words to connect with my brain. "Are ya sure ya don't want to come with us?" he asked. "There's other cat shows."

Other cat shows? What was he talking about?

Holy moly. He was asking me to miss the Cool-Cat Cat Show and go to DizzyPark on Sunday. When I heard that, I forgot about being scared. I couldn't possibly be scared of anybody that stupid. Didn't he realize I'd been prepping Regina for, like, *ever*?

"The cat show's important to me, Mr. Barkenfalt."

"Well, I admire a girl who sticks to her guns," he said. "And please, don't call me Mr. Barkenfalt. Can't we come up with somethin' else?"

I shrugged. Then, at last, he stepped aside. A minute later, my heart was still thudding, but I was safe in my room.

I closed the door, then I took a deep breath, and it was like the air puffed me all up: I had done something brave! I wasn't a wimp after all!

A few minutes ago, my whole world had been kerflooey. A few seconds ago, my life was in danger. Now I felt terrific. Tomorrow, Grandma would see how yuk-o Jimmy Barkenfalt really was, and I would groom my feline queen so perfectly she'd win a blue ribbon for sure.

It is sort of impossible to pat your own self on the back, so I grinned at the ceiling instead. Soon, everything would be back to normal. And it was all because of me.

Chapter Eighteen

At first, the plan worked even better than I'd hoped—too well. Jimmy Barkenfalt sneezed so loud and so often he kept everybody awake.

"It came on suddenly," my grandmother was saying the next morning when I stumbled down the stairs and into the kitchen. "I've never seen a cold like it."

"Doesn't he want any breakfast?" My dad was breaking eggs into a bowl. Mom and the nuisance were still in bed.

"He says he doesn't feel well enough to come down yet," Grandmother said. She was wearing a bright pink bathrobe, no earrings. It was the first time I ever saw her without earrings. I sneaked a look under the table. Her slippers were white and fuzzy, but at least they didn't have bunny ears.

From upstairs came the sound of a colossal sneeze. I had to clench my teeth to keep from laughing. "I guess it's pretty yuk-o, sleeping in the same bed with somebody who has a disgusting cold like that." I tried to sound sympathetic.

"Not so 'yuk-o,'" she said. "Your grandfather used to break out in hives whenever he had an important patient. He'd scratch like a dog with fleas. Now *that* was yuk-o."

This was not what I wanted to hear. But I didn't give up. "Still," I insisted, "red runny nose, itchy eyes, and sniffling and sneezing and . . . uh, blowing your nose, and you know, getting *puffy* and coughing and uh . . . there's all that *snot,* not to mention *mucous* and *phlegm* and—"

"Molly!" my dad interrupted. "Excuse me, but I'm making scrambled eggs here."

My grandmother smiled a sleepy smile. "You know the truth, dear? Once you've taken care of a few children, it takes more than snot to gross you out."

I couldn't believe it. I'd come up with a genius plan. I'd risked my life to carry it out. And she was telling me it was all for nothing because grandmas can't be grossed out? I didn't think my elegant

grandmother knew words like "snot" and "gross-
out"!

"Actually," she was saying, "Jimmy was awfully
sweet. I brought him a cup of tea, and he made a
fuss like it was the last tea on earth. I loved your
grandfather, of course, but it is nice to be shown a
little gratitude. I remember one time . . ."

My mom came down the stairs then. She was
still wearing her bathrobe, and she hadn't brushed
her hair. She collapsed in a kitchen chair and
leaned her head on her hand. Grandma nodded
good morning, but kept on with her story.

". . . seven cookbooks! And all he could think
about was the spot on his tie. Well, I decided then
and there he could learn to make baked Alaska
himself. I wasn't making another one."

"Did he?" Dad offered Mom a plate of eggs, but
she shook her head. She had a scowl on her face. I
figured she was grumpy from not sleeping.

"Did he what?" Grandma asked.

"Did he learn to make baked Alaska?"

Grandma giggled. "Don't be silly. That man
wouldn't—"

"That's enough." Mom's voice was low, but I
knew she was furious. She sounded the way she
did yesterday when she saw the spelling test.
Daddy and Grandma and I got real quiet—scared

quiet. *"I'll thank you to show some respect for my father."*

Grandma's face chewed up about a thousand zillion emotions before it got to mad. "We were married forty-two years, Lila. And I hope I never failed to show your father the respect he was due." She paused, and for a sec it looked like the whole thing might end there. But then she had to go and say, "I only wish he had extended me the same courtesy."

"What's that supposed to mean?" Mom pounced like Regina on a bug.

"Ladies . . . ladies . . ." Daddy tried to butt in, but they were off. It was like they decided to say every nasty thing they'd ever thought about each other. And their voices weren't low, either. Instead of the usual stomping and glaring, my family had started to yell. The words flew so fast, I couldn't catch them all:

". . . always sided with him, ever since you were a little girl . . ." That was my grandmother.

". . . more interested in playing bridge than in what we had to eat in the house . . ." My mother.

". . . didn't bother to tell *me* when Don asked you to get married . . ." Grandma again.

". . . show up out of a clear blue sky and expect me to drop everything while you *honeymoon* . . ." Mom.

". . . made us feel unwelcome ever since we arrived—my only daughter, and . . ." Grandma.

Then, finally, the clincher. "Well, since you were so miserable with Daddy, I hope you and that *vulgarian* will be very happy together." Of course, that was Mom, the English professor. I didn't have a chance to look up "vulgarian" until later, but even at the time I got the idea.

So did Grandma.

Slowly, like a queen in one of her storybooks, she stood up, nodded at my dad, nodded at me, and walked out of the room.

Mom looked like a rag doll after a dog chews it, half the insides gone. After a minute, she mumbled, "I'm going to take a shower." Then she slouched away.

Daddy sighed and looked down at me. "Want some cold eggs?"

Chapter Nineteen

I ate two bites to make Daddy feel better. Sliding down, the eggs felt exactly like the rubber ones that come with a little-kid kitchen set. I pushed the plate away and went to find Regina.

Mom and Grandma had been mad at each other for days; everyone could see that. But this was way worse. They had actually yelled. And the things they said were terrible. I didn't see how they would ever forgive each other. And like everything else that had gone wrong lately, it was all because of Jimmy Barkenfalt.

"Regina? Kitty, kitty?" I called. It was probably good that I had the Cool-Cat Cat Show tomorrow. Grooming Regina would take my mind off my family. After all, those judges were going to examine every hair.

I'd start by washing and rinsing her, then I'd blow her dry, clean out her ears, polish her teeth, and sculpt her claws. Finally, I'd go at her with the brush and comb.

"Kitty, kitty?" Regina was not in the kitty condo. She was not in the Tupperware cupboard. She was not on the nuisance's bed.

Holy moly. First my genius plan is a flop, then Mom and Grandmother practically obliterate each other. Now, on the day before the most important day of her life, Regina pulls her famous disappearing act.

Things couldn't get worse, could they?

Yes.

I was looking for Regina behind the toilet when I heard some kind of fuss by the front door. What now?

"But you *can't* leave! I'm sure Jimmy doesn't feel well enough to travel, and . . ." Mom was standing there in her bathrobe, with her hair dripping.

"I didn't think Jimmy's health would concern you." Grandma was on the bottom step, holding her suitcase. A sneeze from up above announced that Jimmy Barkenfalt was on his way down, too.

"Look, Mother—*Mom*—I didn't mean those things I said. Truly." My mom had the same shamed expression Regina gets after she's thrown up on the rug.

"Yes, you did. And so did I," Grandma said. Her earrings were shaped like bananas. She looked perfectly calm.

"Don't go! Don't go! Don't go!" The nuisance, still in his pajamas, was clinging to Jimmy Barkenfalt's knee. They were standing on the top step, and Jimmy Barkenfalt was trying to lug the suitcases, too.

"*Aaaaaaaaaah-choo!* The sneeze threw Jimmy Barkenfalt off balance, and for a second I thought the whole bunch was going to bumpety-bump down the stairs. But my dad came up behind and grabbed the nuisance, and Jimmy Barkenfalt straightened himself out. "*Aaaaaaaaaah-choo!* Thanks."

This was all wrong. My plan was supposed to separate Grandma from Jimmy Barkenfalt, not separate Grandma from *us.*

Then I looked at Jimmy Barkenfalt's red, puffed-up, sniffly face. He's a drug lord, I reminded myself. He's ruining my family.

But none of those thoughts made me feel better. He looked miserable and sick, and I had done it.

So maybe I deserved it. The catastrophe that came next, I mean. It started when the nuisance tried to block the doorway. The suitcases were already on the front porch. Dad was shaking hands with Jimmy Barkenfalt. Grandmother was bending down to kiss the nuisance good-bye. But the nuisance wouldn't let her go, and the door stayed open. There was a flash of white fur, and Regina was gone again.

Chapter Twenty

Jimmy Barkenfalt had the best shot. She ran right between his legs. He knocked his knees together, but they only caught the tip of her tail, and she pulled it free.

"She'll get in the shrubs! We'll never find her!" I cried.

But I was wrong. Regina ignored the shrubs and dashed across the front yard to the sidewalk. A truck was coming down the street. I was terrified she would dash in front of it, but instead she made a great leap at the elm tree and scampered up the trunk.

If the crows didn't like squirrels in their elm tree, they *really* didn't like a big fluffy feline queen in it. In about ten seconds, every crow in the neighborhood had flown in to torment her. They were cawing almost as loudly as I was hollering. "Come down, kitty, kitty. *Please.* I'll buy you catnip; *please* come down! Your *ribbon!*"

The good-byes were forgotten. Mom ran in the house and came out dressed, with a towel around her wet hair. Soon, everybody was standing on the sidewalk under the elm tree, making suggestions about how to get Regina down.

"Put a dish of cat food at the bottom," said Dad.

"How about the hose?" said Mom.

"Just wait. She'll come down on her own," said Grandma.

Jimmy Barkenfalt, in the meantime, had disappeared. I figured he was gulping Dimetapp in the house, but then I saw him coming toward us from down the block. He was waving at a truck—the same truck I had thought might mow down Regina. The truck was backing toward us, *beep-beep-beep.*

"What's he *doing?*" Mom said. Grandma just smiled.

"How are you with heights?" Jimmy Barkenfalt hollered to my dad.

This was the first funny thing Mom and I had heard in a while. We tried to be nice and stifle our laughter, but some of it spat out. Daddy hesitated, looked at his shoes, looked up into the tree, gulped, and said, "Terrified."

"Well, I guess that beats scared-to-death, which is how I am." Jimmy Barkenfalt blew his red nose into a purple handkerchief. "This guy's a window washer—got an extension ladder on his truck. See it there? Just a lucky thing I noticed as he went by—if lucky's the right word. Ya really want her back, huh?" he asked me.

I nodded.

Jimmy Barkenfalt sneezed and blew his nose again. "You any good with heights?"

Mom answered for both of us. "I'm afraid it's a family trait."

"I'll get 'er!" the nuisance piped up.

Jimmy Barkenfalt grinned and ruffled his hair. "You're braver'n any of us. But that furball weighs more'n you, don't she?"

"Can't we ask *him* to get Regina?" I nodded at the window washer. He was stretching the ladder out against the elm tree.

"There's something called an insurance company," Daddy explained, "and I don't think they'd go for it."

"All ready." The window washer grinned at Jimmy Barkenfalt, who made a face.

"Are you sure you're up to this, sweetie?" Grandma asked.

Jimmy Barkenfalt looked up into the tree like he was thinking, No way. But what he said was, "No sweat." Then he looked at me. "Tell ya the truth, I feel better out here in the open air. Now for how come would that be?"

I swallowed hard. He couldn't possibly have guessed the truth, could he?

"If I'm not back by sundown, send in the Marines . . . or maybe"—Jimmy Barkenfalt looked up again—"maybe the Air Force."

Then he grabbed a rung and started climbing.

Chapter Twenty-one

The ladder shivered with every step. When Jimmy Barkenfalt's shoes were just above our heads, he sneezed a huge sneeze, and the ladder jerked.

Grandma gasped; my heart went *thud*.

"Whoa!" The window washer yanked the ladder straight. "Steady now. Y'okay up there?"

Jimmy Barkenfalt didn't answer. He had caught hold of a branch to keep from falling. Now he sneezed, climbed up one rung, sneezed, and climbed another. In a minute, his sneezing fit was over, and he was climbing fast—faster than I would've thought he could make his body go. I had the feeling it was fear that made him move like that. He didn't want time to think about what he was doing.

I took a couple of good breaths so my heart would quiet down. Two red leaves fluttered into my face, and I brushed them away. I guess I should have been feeling terribly guilty about that booby-trapped pillow, and grateful that Jimmy Barkenfalt was willing to do this for me. But I was too anxious about Regina, and our blue ribbon, to think of those things.

Regina had climbed about halfway up the tree to begin with, but now she kept going higher, trying to get away. Soon there were too many leaves in the way for me to see her.

Nobody said anything, and the wait seemed like a thousand zillion lifetimes. Then I heard an angry *mreeeeo-o-o-ow,* and a hurricane seemed to blow up in the treetop: Crows went crazy; leaves flew; the ladder rocked, so Daddy and the window washer both had to hold on.

"*AAAAAaaaaaaaarrrrgh,* whoa, *nellie-e-e-e-e*—that *hurt!*" Jimmy Barkenfalt yelled, and Regina answered him with a fierce *mreeeeoo-o-o-ow!*

"Sweetie, are you all right?" Grandma's voice was only a whisper.

Now, even the crows got quiet. I stood there with my heart thudding, half expecting this huge man-body to come crashing through the branches, followed by a little cat-body. But then Jimmy Barkenfalt called, "I got her—sort of."

I was so relieved, tears puddled up in my eyes.

Everybody applauded, even the window washer.

But we should've been worried about that "sort of."

The trip down was faster than the trip up. Soon Jimmy Barkenfalt's feet were coming through the leaves. Then he was back on the ground. He was facing away from Grandma, my mom, and me. At first we couldn't see what was making the nuisance's mouth gape while my dad turned pale.

"Jimmy, my gosh, your *face*—let me get antiseptic. I better call the emergency room, an ambulance—my *goodness* . . ."

"What is it?" my grandmother said. "Oh, my stars in heaven!"

Jimmy Barkenfalt turned around, and, I kid you not, his cheek had been shredded. Blood dripped from his jaw; one eye was swelling. He looked so terrible, I actually forgot about Regina till he held her out to me. "Your cat, Little Missy."

She didn't struggle when I pulled her close. When I looked down, I saw she was spattered with blood. It took a second before I realized the blood belonged to Jimmy Barkenfalt. I started to tell him thank you, but before I could, he stumbled. Mom and Grandma grabbed his elbows just as his knees gave way.

Wwwweeeeeeee-o-o-o-o-o-orrrrr. At first I didn't connect the sound of the siren with what was happening in front of me. But it turned out the window washer had used his cell phone to call an ambulance.

While the wail approached, Mom and Grandma helped Jimmy Barkenfalt down to the grass, where he slumped against the trunk of the elm tree. Daddy ran into the house and got some gauze. It was blood soaked the second Jimmy Barkenfalt pressed it to his cheek.

"Just a scratch," he mumbled.

When the ambulance pulled up—lights flashing and siren screaming—the nuisance was so excited he practically bounced off the sidewalk.

The ambulance jerked to a stop, the doors flew open, and three guys sprang out, ready for action.

"How are ya, buddy?" The one in charge crouched next to Jimmy Barkenfalt. "Woozy? Did ya pass out? Nasty cut. What happened here?"

Jimmy Barkenfalt closed his eyes. I think he was overwhelmed. Daddy looked pretty pale himself, but he did his best to explain about Regina and the tree. Then Jimmy Barkenfalt flapped his hand to wave everybody away. "I'm okay. I'm fine." But he didn't seem very fine. It wasn't only the blood. His skin was white and clammy. His voice was shaky.

"We wanna make darn sure o' that, buddy," the ambulance guy said. Then he turned back to Daddy. "How old a gent have we got here?"

Daddy looked at Grandma, who answered, "Sixty-seven."

"Any heart history?"

"None that I know of," she said.

The guy faced his crew, and suddenly it was like watching soldiers in some war movie. "Okay, let's get oxygen going. And I want an EKG. I'll start the IV. *Now, move it!*"

The three guys swarmed over poor Jimmy Barkenfalt. In no time, he was flat on a stretcher, his shirt ripped open to expose his white belly. Three wires ran from a machine to disks stuck on his hairy chest. A clear mask covered his nose and mouth, and there was a pipe like an elephant's trunk that connected it to a green tank. A tube was stuck in his arm, its other end attached to a bag of clear liquid hanging off a pole.

The two crew guys lifted the stretcher into the ambulance while the one in charge talked into his phone. "We're on our way with a sixty-seven-year-old man, no known cardiac history, BP one-sixty over ninety, pulse ninety-five. Sustained cat scratch in a tree, near-syncopal event, ETA eight minutes . . . Roger. Ten-four and out."

Wwwweeeeeo-o-o-o-o-orrrrr. The siren cranked up, the lights flashed, and the ambulance sped away. It had all happened in a blur. Now I was left with a terrible picture in my head: Jimmy Barkenfalt, all fragile and helpless on the stretcher, wires and tubes stuck everyplace like he'd been trapped by some spidery machine.

"You coming, Molly?" Daddy's hand touched my shoulder. "Molly?"

"What? Oh—the emergency room. But Regina . . ." She lay limp in my arms, panting. While the ambulance was here, I had hardly thought about her, but now I saw I couldn't leave her. She didn't look so good herself.

"Okay, princess. You see to your cat. We'll let you know as soon as we hear anything."

The window washer was pulling away from the curb. He raised his hand to Daddy as Daddy jogged toward our car in the driveway. Mom, Grandma, and the nuisance were already strapped in.

Chapter Twenty-Two

In the house, I put Regina down in her kitty bed and sat on the floor next to her. My heart was still thudding from excitement, and all these emotions shot round and round inside me. I was relieved to have Regina back; that was the only good one.

The worst one was guilt. Had the allergic reaction made Jimmy Barkenfalt weak? So when he climbed the tree he got sick? And hadn't he climbed the tree for me—to rescue *my* cat?

I felt guilty, and I felt scared—scared Jimmy Barkenfalt might not be all right. Scared somebody would find out what I'd done, and I'd be in trouble like I couldn't even imagine.

There was something else, too. It wasn't nice. I didn't even want to admit I felt it. But it was in there, shooting around with the relief and the guilt and the fear: anger.

I had done something incredibly mean to Jimmy Barkenfalt, and he had done something incredibly generous for me—but I was still mad at him. And some part of me still blamed him for everything that had gone wrong, even for his being sick now. None of it would have happened, *none of it,* if he had just stayed in Florida where he belonged.

I sat there on the floor and looked inside myself and saw somebody I didn't recognize. She wasn't the good kid that grown-ups like. She was somebody really bad, who deserved to be in a lot of trouble—if anybody ever found out what she had done.

My mind is one of the mysteries of my life. One minute, I was sitting on the floor discovering what an awful person I am. The next, I was thinking about the Cool-Cat Cat Show. Maybe it was just habit. After all, I had been planning for the Cool-Cat Cat Show since long before I'd even heard of Jimmy Barkenfalt.

I looked down at Regina. She was asleep. Her chest rose and fell, like running up an entire elm tree had tired her out.

I could scrub the blood off. Regina was exhausted, but there was nothing really wrong with her, was there? And anyway, grooming Regina would take my mind off everything.

I stood up and took the kitty brush from the table. But when I looked at Regina again, something didn't seem right. I stroked her head to tail. She opened her eyes and let out a little warning rumble.

"What is it?" Her paws were fine. And the only blood was Jimmy Barkenfalt's.

I stroked her again. She rumbled again. And that's when I saw it: the droop of her tail. Carefully, I ran my finger along it. About halfway, there was a bump like a knuckle only a whole lot bumpier.

Holy moly. Now the Cool-Cat Cat Show really was history.

Jimmy Barkenfalt had broken Regina's tail.

After everything else, it sort of crushed me. I didn't even cry, just collapsed against the wall and squeezed my eyes shut. I must have been there a long time before Regina startled me with a loud, moaning *mreeeowwwww.*

"What?" I shook my head. "Oh . . . *oh.* Holy moly! It hurts, doesn't it?"

I was not only an awful person, I was a nincompoop. Here was my cat with a broken bone for golly sake, and I was too busy being miserable to do anything about it.

"Stay there! I'll be back!" I told her. I phoned the vet, who said to bring her in right away. I explained how Mom and Dad were gone, and she told me to give Regina a baby aspirin to kill the pain.

"Then keep her comfortable until you can bring her in," she told me.

"Her tail will heal, won't it?" I asked.

"I need to take a look. But she should be okay."

I found the aspirin in the medicine cabinet, spilled one out, and went in to try it on Regina. I had given Regina pills lots of times. How you do it is put the pill on the end of your finger, pinch her mouth open, then stick the pill as far down her throat as you can. Then she fights you and claws you and spits the pill out. Only this time Regina swallowed it on the first try, which seemed like more proof of how bad she felt.

"When your tail heals," I told her, "it's back to the old routine. You're still going to be a champion. You just have to wait a while is all." I guess I was talking to comfort her, or comfort myself. But she opened her blue eyes and glared at me. "Don't you want to be a champion?" I asked.

A few minutes later, the front door opened and the nuisance yelled, "Molly! Molly! Grandpa has to stay in the hospital! Where are you?"

"Regina's room. What—?"

The nuisance ran in, his mouth going as fast as his feet. "They hadda stick him with a needle so many times! Grandma's there, too, and—"

"Stay—?"

"—we hadda come home an' tell you an' get his junk. You oughta see the needles they got! I hope *I* never . . ."

The nuisance couldn't stop talking. I guess this whole thing had been the most excitement of his life.

"It isn't only 'cuz he got scratched. His heart's making the wrong noise, too. It's s'posed to go *bump, bump, bump.* But it goes *bump-bump-bump-bump.* That's what the nice lady told me—"

What was he talking about? I knew Mom and Dad would explain eventually, but right now I could hear them thumping around upstairs.

Finally the nuisance ran out of breath. He took a big wheezing gulp of air, then he gave me a funny look. "Hey, you're pettin' 'er. You never pet 'er. Is she sick, too?"

I was so surprised, I didn't think about the broken tail. "I do, too, pet her!" I said.

"No, you do not. You only brush her an' wash her an' junk. That's how come she doesn't like you."

"She does, too, like me! She's my cat!"

The nuisance shook his head. "And besides, you don't like her, either."

Chapter Twenty-three

Later that afternoon, Mom drove Regina and me to the vet's office. In the examining room, Dr. Eshman looked Regina over and shook her head. "This is an unusual one. Typically, cats break the tip of their tail—slammed in a door, that kind of thing. How did it happen?"

I told how she'd gone up the tree.

"Well, she's a healthy cat," Dr. Eshman said. "You've taken excellent care of her. There shouldn't be any problem. I'll have to keep her at least overnight, though. As soon as I get someone in here to assist, I'll perform the amputation, and—"

"The *what*?" I thought I hadn't heard right.

"I'm sorry, Molly. I should have realized. . . ." She smiled sympathetically. "You see, it's very difficult to splint a cat's tail. Rarely successful, and painful for the cat. A house cat thrives just fine after the surgery. You'll see."

"But I can't show a cat with half a tail!"

"Well, no. But Regina means more to you than ribbons, doesn't she?"

I didn't answer. I was thinking about what the nuisance had said.

The hospital's visiting hours started at 7:00 P.M. The nurses had let Grandma stay in Jimmy Barkenfalt's room all day, but the rest of us could only come in for a little while, and only one at a time. The doctor said Jimmy Barkenfalt needed rest and *positively no more excitement.*

It turned out the nuisance had got it pretty much right when he told me what had happened. Jimmy Barkenfalt's cheek had taken fifteen stitches. That was the needle they stuck him with so many times. And his heart *was* making a funny noise, or anyway, a funny pattern on the machine he was hooked to.

"It's because he's old and fat," the nuisance explained as we walked past the nurse's station.

"*Joey!*" Mom shushed him.

"Well, it *is*."

At the door, Daddy looked at me. "Why don't you go in first, Molly? You haven't seen him yet. And you do want to thank him, after all. We'll wait out here in the hallway. Go on."

I couldn't exactly say no. I'll just tell him thanks and leave, I thought. Say it so fast I don't have a chance to start feeling everything all over again.

I stepped across the threshold and stopped. Propped up on pillows, Jimmy Barkenfalt looked like a small person in a big bed. Half his face was puffed up black and blue, with one eye totally closed. There was a pipe thing coming out of his nose, and wires and tubes attached to his arms and his chest. He looked worse than when the ambulance hauled him away.

I shouldn't have been surprised. If he was fine, he wouldn't be here, would he?

"Who have we here?" Jimmy Barkenfalt turned his head to look at me with his good eye. "Oh. The Little Missy herself. So," he pointed to the black stitches on his cheek, "how do ya like Frankenstein?" His words came out in puffs, like he couldn't catch his breath.

Grandma, sitting in a chair by the bed, shook her head. "He won't stop making jokes. Had the nurses in stitches earlier."

"Your grandma's mixed up." He lay back against the pillows. "I'm the one with all the stitches."

Grandma patted his head. "Why don't you eat something, sweetie?" She surveyed the dinner tray on a cart by his bed. "Hmmmm, well . . . the Jell-O's probably safe."

Jimmy Barkenfalt shook his head. "Never trust no pink foods," he said.

Grandma sighed. "He's a wretched patient. But I love him. Come the rest of the way in, Molly. Sit down if you like."

"Make yourself at home," Jimmy Barkenfalt added.

I walked a few steps toward the bed. Say it quick and get out, I told myself. "I'm not supposed to be here too long. I only wanted to tell you—" I stopped. Somewhere between my brain and my tongue the two words "thank" and "you" got stuck. For a second, I stood there with my mouth open while the entire world watched and waited for me to finish my sentence. Anyway, that's what it felt like.

Then, horrified, I realized my cheeks were wet with tears.

"I'm sorry," I gasped between sobs. "I'm so sorry. It's my fault. . . ."

"Oh, Molly—*no*." Grandma had come over and put her arms around me. My tears soaked into her dress. "All cats climb trees. It's a law of nature."

Jimmy Barkenfalt coughed, and I felt Grandma pull away. "Sweetie—?"

"I'm okay." He cleared his throat. "But that ain't what the little missy means."

My tears stopped like he'd twisted the faucet. *He knew.*

"What?" Grandma walked me to the chair and sat me down. I couldn't look at her or Jimmy Barkenfalt, so I stared at my lap. What would happen to me now?

Chapter Twenty-four

"Go on, Little Missy. Enlighten 'er. Me, too, for that matter. There's a few details I ain't quite got figured."

I didn't think I could find my voice, but then my always mysterious mind thought of something: Stephanie, whose life is in a constant state of busted. Does she whine? Does she make excuses? Does she lie?

No. She's like somebody who rips a Band-Aid off fast. She gets it over with.

So, without once looking up, I told them what I'd done. I started with overhearing the phone call. When I got to the part about cat fur, Grandma's hand slid off my shoulder.

". . . so then, I guess that's how come you got so sick," I said finally. "That's how come you're even here." I took a breath and waited.

Grandma was sitting on the edge of the bed, facing me. "All because you thought he was some kind of *criminal*?"

It sounded crazy when she said it. But I looked up at Jimmy Barkenfalt's ugly stitched-together face, and anger flooded back. I was already in so much trouble, why not say what I really thought?

"And what *about* that phone call, anyway?" I didn't wait for an answer. "Besides, that wasn't all of it. Don't you see, Grandma? He's ruined everything! He broke Regina's tail; he made you and Mom fight, *and* Dad and Mom—he's nothing like Grandfather! He's nothing like any of us! Since you brought him here, everything's kerflooey."

I don't know what I expected exactly. Maybe a slap like Mom gave the nuisance. But what I got from Grandma was even worse: "Well, if Lila hasn't raised a little *snob*—" she began.

But I'll never know what else I am because Jimmy Barkenfalt interrupted with a round of coughing that sounded sick as bones crunching in the garbage disposal.

"*Sweetie?*" Grandma was so scared, she forgot about me. "I'm calling the nurse."

"No, no." Still hacking, Jimmy Barkenfalt held up his hand. "This is just how us old, infirm guys laugh." It was a minute before he could go on, and then the words almost made him cough again. "Kerflooey, huh? 'At's a good one, kid. Didja ever stop to think maybe I been feelin' pretty *kerflooey* myself?"

"Now, now, sweetie, it's just that you're *ill*," Grandma tried to soothe him, but he wouldn't be soothed.

"I mean before that," he snapped. "Ya know, your family ain't exactly a big bowl o' cherries, Little Missy. Ya got a mama acts like the Queen o' Sheba, a dad too scared o' her t'say boo, an' a little brother—well, I admit Joe's okay. But give him time."

Jimmy Barkenfalt squeezed his eyes shut and shifted his weight. Grandma threatened to call the nurse again, but he told her to pipe down. You should've seen the look on her face.

"What I'm gonna say now—I prob'ly got rocks in my head," he grumbled. "Ya like to 'a' *killed* me, Little Missy, and I oughta throw y'outta here on your butt for it. Instead, I'm gonna explain a couple things. You're young yet yourself. Comin' outta that fruitcake family, I dunno, but *maybe* there's a shred o' hope for you, too."

Jimmy Barkenfalt talked, and Grandma fussed: "Now don't exert yourself so. You know they told you not to get excited." But actually, the excitement seemed to do him good. There was some pink coming into his face, and his voice was less pathetic.

"First 'n' number one," he said, "that phone call you spied on? You tell your pal Stephanie she don't know beans about beans. Plenty o' honest guys do business in South America, and I'm one. My interest ain't drugs. It's clothes—polyester mainly. And clothes is what I wanted those bozos to ship to me on time. Capeesh? All on the up and up, Little Missy.

"Number two," he said, "that nasty furball o' yours. As far as breakin' 'er tail, it was the only way t'keep 'er from bashin' her brains into the sidewalk. Not that that furball's *got* much in the way o' brains. Your Regina's so dumb she *dove* outta that tree, and the only part I could grab on to was tail.

"Anyway, she's an ugly furball, am I right? She never woulda won ya no ribbons."

Jimmy Barkenfalt lay back and closed his eyes like such a long speech tired him out.

"*Now,* see what you've done." Grandma scowled at me, ready to pick up where she had left off.

But Jimmy Barkenfalt didn't let her. "Oh, lay off," he said, and his eyes blinked open. Then he took a long, careful deep breath, like he was testing out his lungs. This time he didn't cough. "Know somethin'?" He looked at me. "I feel better. How 'bout you, Little Missy?"

Chapter Twenty-five

"**A** week? *Wicked!*" Stephanie's voice on the phone was approving. "But, hey—wait. It's already started, right?"

"Well, yeah, I guess."

"*Chee-zitz,* Molly! Your parents don't even know how to *ground* a person! They shouldn't go letting you talk on the *phone!*" Stephanie was shaking her head, I could tell.

It was Sunday afternoon, and I had called Stephanie to give her the update. Mom and Dad had grounded me for booby-trapping the pillow, of course. There had been a lively discussion before they came up with that for punishment. I think Grandma favored boiling me in oil.

Anyway, I had plenty to tell Stephanie. When I was done, she claimed she knew all along Jimmy Barkenfalt wasn't a drug lord. "Maybe he's not even pukey," she said. I didn't answer because I was still trying to work that part out.

"But you're not the only one with news, you know," she told me.

That same morning, Stephanie's mom had spotted biker Jerry's name on the honor-roll list they print in the newspaper. He's a straight-A student! Now her mom was practically begging Emily to bring him over to the house.

"Meanwhile, *I* am totally disappointed," Stephanie said. "I mean, some biker dude! If he gets good grades like that, he's nothing but a *fake.*"

It was around two o'clock when Daddy brought Jimmy Barkenfalt home. The doctors said he had made a miraculous recovery. In fact, his heart was pretty strong for somebody his age. His face was going to heal okay, too.

I stayed out of the way while Daddy and Grandma settled Jimmy Barkenfalt back into our house. From my bedroom, I could hear the three of them come up the stairs. Grandma was still fussing. "That's *much* too heavy for you, sweetie!

Don, you take it, won't you? Sweetie, let me fix you
a cup of broth. You must get your strength back."

Jimmy Barkenfalt didn't answer her. Instead, I
heard his gravelly voice ask, "I seen Joe and Lila,
but where's the little missy? Ain't she part o' the
welcoming committee?"

Holy moly. What did he want now?

A second later, Daddy knocked on my door.
"Your presence is requested," he said. Then he
shrugged and whispered, "I don't know either,
princess."

When I walked into their room, Jimmy Barkenfalt was pulling off his shoes, and Grandma was
counting pills out of a little bottle.

"Ya didn't answer me last night," he said without looking up.

"Didn't answer? I—"

"I asked ya did ya feel better, and then Joe
knocked, and your folks bumbled in. We never finished our chat."

Like I've said, the way my mind works is one of
the mysteries of my life. I mean, since the hospital, I'd done practically nothing but think. And
with all that thinking, I had figured a few things
out. Like the nuisance might be a poor, dumb
four-year-old, but he was right about how I treated
Regina.

But was I feeling better? I hadn't thought about that at all. Not till this second, when Jimmy Barkenfalt asked.

"Yeah," I answered. "*Yeah.* I feel a thousand zillion times better."

I did, too. Ever since I'd confessed. It turns out being grounded is better than feeling guilty. Still, I wished Grandma would talk to me.

Jimmy Barkenfalt slid his feet into slippers, then he eased himself into a chair.

"You should be lying down," Grandma said. "Here." She handed him a couple of pills. "These will help you sleep."

"Who wants to sleep?" he asked her.

"The doctor said—"

"Aw, the doctor can take a flying leap. Except for this itty-bitty scratch, I'm fit as a fiddle."

Grandma looked stern, but Jimmy Barkenfalt flashed a grin at her. He had a bandage over his stitches now, so his face looked more like The Mummy than Frankenstein. When he grinned, it was so lopsided and funny, even Grandma had to smile.

"That's better," he said. "This whole fruitcake family o' yours is too serious, am I right? Now, Little Missy, I didn't call you in here for idle chitchat. First of all, I want you should get somethin' outta that pillow before I commence to dyin' again. Capeesh?"

"Oh . . . " I said it like I'd been socked in the stomach. Feeling Grandma's glare burn into me, I walked over to the bed and reached in the pillowcase. "Uh, here." Not thinking, I held the wad of cat fur out to Jimmy Barkenfalt, who waved it away same as a vampire does with a cross. "Oh! Sorry . . . I'll just . . . " I retreated into the hallway and threw the fur away. Then I got a new pillowcase from the linen closet.

"Okay, *that's* settled." Jimmy Barkenfalt took the clean pillowcase. "Second item. You told me the truth last night. It's only right I return the favor."

I had no idea what he was talking about, and I didn't find out soon, either. The phone interrupted, and a minute later Mom was at the guest-room door. "Molly, that was Dr. Eshman."

"How is she? Is her tail really—"

"The surgery went fine. Regina's a tad bit groggy, but she'll mend best at home. Get your coat, and we'll go pick her up."

"Okay, but—" I looked at Jimmy Barkenfalt.

"It'll wait," he said. "Give my regards to the furball."

Even though I knew what the vet had done, I was shocked. Regina looked pathetic. She had about half a tail left, but that half had been shaved for the surgery. So instead of the proud, fluffy white plume I was used to, my pedigreed Persian had what looked like a naked rat tail attached to her rear end.

Sometimes my mind is not that mysterious. A song immediately popped into my head: "Three Blind Mice."

"Now, bring her back in a couple of days," Dr. Eshman was saying, "so I can change the dressing. All she needs is baby aspirin for pain. And don't worry. The fur will grow back."

I tried not to look at Regina too much as I carried her out to the car. She was so ugly and strange. Was the nuisance right about that, too? Didn't I even like my own cat?

"Go ahead and hold her, Molly." Mom opened the door for me. "It's too cruel to put the poor thing in her carrier." So with Regina in my lap, I strapped myself into the backseat. Mom got in and started the car. She hadn't said much on the way to Dr. Eshman's office. When we turned onto the highway, I worked up my nerve and asked, "Are you still mad at me?"

She looked at me in the rearview mirror. "About the pillow? No. I never was."

"You weren't?"

"Truthfully, I wanted to do the same thing myself," she said.

"*You* wanted to put cat hair in Jimmy Barkenfalt's pillow?"

Mom laughed a real laugh, not the drama-class kind. "Not precisely, Molly. But I didn't like Jimmy, either. I felt like doing something *mean*."

"But you didn't."

"Not to Jimmy. But remember when I spanked Joey? I think I wanted to spank somebody else. By now, I should've learned to pick on people my own size."

I thought of the family hug in Regina's room and how good it made me feel. "The nuisance forgave you," I said.

"He did," Mom said. "I just haven't forgiven myself."

We rode in silence for a few minutes. I had been petting Regina, and now I stole a glance down at her. She was asleep, and her flat little Persian face was as sweet as ever. "I'm going to be nicer to her now that she's just my cat, not a future blue-ribbon winner," I told Mom. "It's weird, but I think she might be happier this way."

"What about you?" Mom asked.

"I don't know. Maybe I'll be bored."

We were coming to a red light, and Mom put her foot on the brake. "I might go back to work," she said.

I thought I must have missed something. "Weren't we talking about Regina?"

Mom looked at me in the mirror. "Ever since the uh . . . *incident* with Joey, I've been thinking, Molly. Did it ever occur to you that perhaps I've treated you the same way you've treated Regina? As if it weren't enough to be Molly Knight, you also had to be—"

"—some future blue-ribbon winner." I finished her sentence.

"Indeed."

I stroked Regina and considered. Then I smiled. "*Hey,* are you saying I don't have to get straight As anymore?"

Mom didn't hesitate. "I'll still expect straight As. You're smart, Molly. Never sell yourself short. But you should also know that I'd love you even if you failed fifth grade. You do know that, don't you?"

I looked at Regina again, and this time I kept looking. She was pathetic, but she was my cat. "Yeah, Mom," I said. "And I love you, too. Even though you're hyper."

We were only a block from our house. Regina had fallen asleep. I felt cozy in the car, comfortable and warm with Mom there, my cat asleep in my lap, and "Three Blind Mice" playing in my head.

Chapter Twenty-six

Grandma and Jimmy Barkenfalt stayed the whole next week with us. Everybody got along a lot better, and all sorts of other stuff happened.

Mom phoned her old boss, the dean, and she'll be teaching part-time, starting after Christmas.

The nuisance came home from preschool Tuesday with a big black eye. Ethan J., world's biggest bully, had punched him for swiping the magenta crayon. At first the nuisance was embarrassed, but then Jimmy Barkenfalt told him they could be monsters together. After that, the nuisance kept looking at himself in the mirror and snarling.

I think Ethan J. better watch out.

On Wednesday after work, Daddy brought home two heads of iceberg lettuce from the supermarket and announced he was putting his foot down. He would never eat another leaf of arugula as long as he lived. There was a lively discussion, but in the end Mom said okay. From now on, Daddy's going to make the salads.

Likewise, with Mom going to work, I'm supposed to start helping around the house more. My first assignment was to clean out the Tupperware cupboard. You should've seen the cat hair. Yuk-o!

On Friday, I aced the spelling test. Mom and Dad decided even though I was grounded, I could go to DizzyPark with the family the next day.

Of course, Stephanie was disgusted.

And actually, being grounded wasn't that bad. It gave me extra thinking time. I spent it totaling up all the good stuff that had happened since Jimmy Barkenfalt came, and all the bad stuff.

There was a lot: Mom drama-class fainting, my grandmother giggling, me doing something bad but not wimpy, Mom spanking the nuisance and hugging everybody, Regina getting a rat's tail. . . .

What I decided was this: It isn't always bad if somebody spins the dials and makes your life ker-flooey. Sometimes when you get the focus back, things look better than they used to.

. . .

I never noticed before, but DizzyPark has a Tunnel of Love. You can check it out if you go there. It's sort of by the baby roller coaster and the Ferris wheel.

Ever since Grandma married Jimmy Barkenfalt, she's been crazy about Tunnels of Love. So she dragged us over there first thing Saturday morning. We were the only ones in line for it. I guess people into serious smooching—teenagers, yuk-*o*—wait till it's dark.

The little red boats have pink hearts all over them. They're supposed to be for a couple, but if you squeeze, you can get three people in. I squashed between Grandma and Jimmy Barkenfalt in the first boat. The nuisance was between Mom and Dad behind us.

The guy in charge of the ride looped a belt over us, pulled a lever, and called, *"Au revoir!"* Then we floated into a plastic tunnel. I could hear the nuisance whining behind us, "Yuk-*o*!" while Mom shushed him. "We'll do the roller coaster next. I promise."

Inside it was dark, and goopy violin music was playing. Every now and then there was a pink or a red light aimed at some Valentine scene on the wall: cupids shooting arrows at us, silhouettes of people kissing, girls making goo-goo eyes at boys making goo-goo eyes back.

If you ask me, the nuisance was right.

Anyway, Jimmy Barkenfalt had his arm across me and around Grandma. I was afraid any second he might lean over and nuzzle her, but he didn't. Instead he asked did I remember last week when he had something to tell me.

"Oh yeah. When I had to go get Regina. What was it?"

Grandma giggled. "It's a good one," she said. I looked into her face. In the dim light, I could just make out her palm-tree earrings. Even after this whole week, she hadn't officially forgiven me.

"For a smart girl, Little Missy, you been dumb about one thing," Jimmy Barkenfalt said. "Didn't you ever wonder for how come I'd risk my neck in a tree for your furball? When you was the one made me sick as a dog?"

"I dunno. I guess I just figured you were really nice."

"Ha!" Grandma laughed.

"I *am* nice." Jimmy Barkenfalt sounded hurt.

"Not *that* nice," she said.

Now he grinned. The big bandage had been replaced by a regular Band-Aid, so he looked pretty normal. "Nah," he admitted. "Not *that* nice. At any rate, Little Missy, till you went and spilled your guts at the hospital, I had no idea what it was you'd done in our room that night. All I knew was you'd been on the bed. I knew that 'cuz you closed my magazine, remember? And naturally I suspicioned you were up to no good. But my point is this: You coulda gone to your grave with nobody the wiser."

Grandma giggled again.

"But you *said*—" I started to argue.

"Did not."

I thought back to the conversation that night and got mad all over again. "You *tricked* me!"

"In a manner o' speaking, yes," he said.

If I hadn't been trapped between them in a little boat in a Tunnel of Love, I would've turned my back and stalked off. As it was, I folded my arms over my chest and pouted. The goopy violin music played on and on.

"Molly?" Grandma's voice was gentle. "I think maybe you wanted to tell the truth."

"So you could call me a snob?"

"You are a snob," she said.

"Grandma!"

"Well, you are. I was, too, for almost sixty-five years. But I got over it. If we're lucky, someday even your mother might get over it."

It didn't take a genius to know this was her way of forgiving me. It wasn't a terribly polite way, but it would do.

"There's still one thing I haven't figured out," I said.

"What's that?" Jimmy Barkenfalt asked.

"What am I supposed to call you? What you are really is my stepgrandpa."

"Sounds like a villain in one of my old story-books," said Grandma.

"So," I said, "I had this idea just now. You're not my real grandpa, and you're not my stepgrandpa; you must be my Polyester Grandpa."

Grandma giggled, and Jimmy Barkenfalt spat out a guffaw that echoed round the walls of the plastic tunnel. Then suddenly we floated into the light, and for a second the world was a big bright blur.

"Sounds pretty good," Jimmy Barkenfalt said at last. "But plain ol' Grandpa's better for everyday, am I right?"

About the Author

Martha Freeman is the author of *Stink Bomb Mom,* a humorous novel for children and of *The Year My Parents Ruined My Life,* a comic novel for young adults. She wrote and edited hundreds of articles for newspapers and magazines before tiring of real life and turning to fiction. A native Californian, she now lives in State College, Pennsylvania, with her husband and three children.